PURRFE

THE MYSTER

NIC SAINT

PURRFECT FURY

The Mysteries of Max 62

Illustrations by Mark Beech
Edited by Chereese Graves

www.nicsaint.com

Give feedback on the book at: info@nicsaint.com

facebook.com/nicsaintauthor
@nicsaintauthor

First Edition

Printed in the U.S.A

INTRODUCTION

MAX

DOOLEY

HARRIET

BRUTUS

ODELIA KINGSLEY

CHASE KINGSLEY

MARGE POOLE

TEX POOLE

UNCLE ALEC

VESTA MUFFIN

PURRFECT FURY

My Kingdom for a Cat!

Look, I don't mind the occasional house guest. After all, cats are well-known for their hospitality. Okay, maybe that's not entirely true, but when a woman moved in and immediately announced she was allergic to cats and induced Odelia to kick us all out of the house, I admit I wasn't happy about it. And then when Chase was taken to the hospital suffering from a mysterious ailment at the same time as the four of us came down with a weird rash, it was enough to cause me to worry.

And this was even before the strange events began in earnest. Burglars, spies and other denizens of the underworld suddenly circled our home—that technically wasn't our home anymore. Suffice it to say I was starting to feel the heat!

CHAPTER 1

Mike Knight stared at the woman standing in front of him. The things she just told him had come as a complete surprise. "You can't be serious," he said.

"Oh, but I am," she confirmed. "Dead serious."

He shook his head. It's one thing for a family to harbor a secret, but another to discover that secret.

"Nobody ever told me I had a cousin."

"Nobody told me either. Until my grandmother died."

"My dad will be devastated to discover that his grandfather was cheating on his grandmother with another woman."

"How do you think I felt when Gran told me? It's one of those secrets nobody likes to know about. The ones best kept hidden along with the other skeletons in the family closet."

He eyed the woman keenly. Francine Martin was an attractive woman his own age, stylishly dressed in a camel-colored coat, cashmere turtleneck sweater and gray slacks. When she contacted his office she had introduced herself as a consultant for a marketing firm based in San Francisco, where her family originated from. Refusing to communicate through a middleman she had insisted on talking to him personally, announcing she had something very important but also very personal to tell him. His interest piqued, they had exchanged emails, and that's when she had revealed the stunning truth that his great-grandfather and hers were one and the same person. According to her information Ebenezer Knight was a bigamist and had married two different women and started two separate families in different states.

And that wasn't the only shocking piece of news she had to impart. There was more—much more.

Before agreeing to meet his distant cousin face to face, he had told her no one in his family was to find out. At least until he could verify the veracity of her claim. So when she proposed the old potash mine his family owned as their meeting place, he had readily agreed. Which is why they now stood facing each other for the very first time, in the mine that had once secured Mike's family's fortune. The mine had been opened and operated by Ebenezer Knight himself many years ago, but now lay derelict.

"You said you had something else you wanted to tell me," he reminded her. "Something even more shocking than the truth about our ancestor? Though I can't imagine what could be more shocking than the fact that old Ebenezer was a two-timing scoundrel."

"When my grandmother died, she left me a small legacy, since I was her only granddaughter. My parents both passed away when I was very young, and I was raised by my grandmother. So we were always very close. Part of this legacy was a box of some personal items she had always kept in the attic. And in this box was a diary belonging to her father."

"A diary written by Ebenezer Knight?" asked Mike with a frown.

"That's right. Apparently it was part of a set of diaries, but unfortunately I have no idea what happened to the rest. It's possible they were destroyed or lost. But in the diary my grandmother kept, Ebenezer described how he purchased the piece of land that would later become this very mine we're standing in right now. At the time potash was a very lucrative substance, and he'd go on to make a fortune."

"Potash is still a lucrative business," Mike pointed out. "Unfortunately they exhausted the mine years ago. Whatever is left isn't worth digging up now, so the mine was closed back when my dad was in charge of the company. This must have been in the late eighties as far as I can remember."

"What if I told you that there's something else in this mine. Something that's even more lucrative than potash?" Francine's eyes were glittering when she spoke these words, and Mike couldn't help but be intrigued all over again.

"What do you mean? My dad said the mine was completely exhausted. Nothing left to dig up."

"That's not what our common ancestor's diary says. There's something else here, Mike. Lithium."

"Lithium?"

Francine nodded. "Potash and lithium are often found in the same deposits."

"I know, but there was never any lithium found here. And I'm sure my dad had the best experts going all over the property before he declared it derelict and decided to abandon it."

There had been many plans over the years to develop the land, but lack of funds—and perhaps a lack of vision—had caused those plans never to pan out. So now the plot of land just lay there, which was a waste. Recently they'd found a developer willing to take it off their hands, and preliminary contracts had been drawn up. If what Francine was saying was true, they might be able to reopen the mine, and turn it profitable again.

"Clearly you haven't been digging in the right place," said

Francine with a shrug. "Because in his diary our great-grandfather definitely mentions lithium. Though at the time it wasn't considered profitable. Now it's the new gold rush, of course, since they use lithium to produce the batteries in electric vehicles. They simply can't dig up enough of the stuff."

Mike swallowed. Lithium. If this was true it would be the answer to his prayers. A possibility to rebuild his family's fortune and add a lot more to it than ever before. In recent years his fortunes had been reversed, and even though he'd never admit it to Francine, he was hanging on by his fingernails.

"If what you're saying is true," he said, his voice suddenly hoarse. "That would be huge."

"I told you," she said cheerfully.

"So this diary… it pinpoints the exact location of the lithium deposits?"

"It does. It even contains a map."

"And this deposit, it's part of the original mine? I mean, do we already own the land?"

"You do own the land, Mike. All you have to do is to start digging. Provided you know where, of course."

Inadvertently he glanced around, at the old deserted shacks which once were a beehive of activity. It wouldn't be all that difficult to restart operations. With his dad's experience it wouldn't be hard at all.

"So this diary…"

"Fifty-fifty, Mike," said Francine. "And a finder's fee for the diary itself."

"Fifty-fifty?"

"For whatever proceeds you end up getting out of this newly established lithium mine. If it wasn't for me, you wouldn't even know about the lithium, and that money would be gone. So it only seems right that I get my fair share of the profits. And besides, while your side of the family prospered, mine didn't, since Ebenezer eventually divorced my great-grandmother and deserted her, leaving her to raise their child all by herself. So I think you'll agree that your family owes my family for what Ebenezer did to us, Mike."

He nodded. "I'd have to see the diary, of course. And determine its authenticity. And then I'd have to bring in experts to locate this lithium deposit and figure out potential profitability and feasibility."

"Fifty-fifty, Mike. And a finder's fee when I hand over the diary."

"How much?" he asked quickly.

"A hundred thousand."

He gulped a little. But he was too much of a businessman not to see the potential here. "Done," he said. "Providing the diary is genuine."

"Oh, I can assure you that it is."

He stared at her. She hadn't lied. The things she had told him were pretty shocking. But if they were true they could transform his entire future and that of his family. Wait till he told his dad, he thought. He'd be even more surprised than he was, since he was the one who had operated this mine all those years.

"Okay, so how do we proceed?" he asked, putting his business cap firmly back on. Francine might be family, but clearly she was approaching this meeting from a strictly business point of view.

"I'm going to be in town for the next couple of days. So you talk to whoever you need to talk to, and we'll arrange a second meeting. You bring in an expert and I'll produce the diary. The expert makes sure the diary is the real deal, and then we negotiate a timetable." She flashed a devastating smile at him, which told him she was probably extremely good at what she did. "So looks like we're in business… cousin?"

"Looks like we are," he confirmed, holding out his hand and giving hers a vigorous shake. "Cousin."

* * *

What neither Mike nor Francine knew was that their secret meeting wasn't so secret at all. From the top of a hill he and Francine had been watched by a very interested party, who had snapped quite a few high-quality shots and video footage of the pair. With binoculars trained on the scion of the Knight family, the mysterious observer now saw how Mike picked up a rock and studied it for a moment before throwing it into the deep pit that was a remnant of the excavating activities that had once been carried out there.

Pity the unseen spy couldn't hear what the cousins were actually discussing down there. But the simple fact that Mike Knight and Francine Martin were meeting in secret told him all he needed to know.

He watched as Mike crawled back into his Mercedes, and soon was off at a fast clip, the tires of his sleek silver vehicle spitting up sand and debris as he roared away. Moments later he was followed by a second Mercedes, this one a dark maroon convertible driven by Francine.

The spy didn't waste time sending the images and footage he shot to his contact.

The instructions came back fast and furious, and he grimaced when he read them.

Clearly the time for playing games was over. Things were heating up!

* * *

Francine fingered the amulet that was dangling from her rearview mirror. A present from her beloved grandmother, it had been a fixture in every car she had ever owned, even in the rental she was now driving. Gran had told her the amulet would protect her, and even though she wasn't an overly superstitious person, its presence was oddly reassuring. She knew she needed all the protection she could harness. Ever since she had come forward with the diary and contacted Mike Knight, certain forces had been unleashed that would stop at nothing to thwart her plans. She expertly steered the car from the old mine's dusty road onto the asphalt track that led into town. And she had just reached the intersection when a black sedan suddenly veered onto the road behind her and drove up. The game was on.

She wondered how they had found her so quickly, but then figured these people probably had their spies everywhere. As the sedan clung to her rear, a sliver of fear ran through her, and she took a firmer grip on the wheel. It was an unremarkable sedan, and try as she might, she couldn't get a good view of its driver. All she could see was that it was probably a man and that he was wearing dark shades.

They weren't even trying to hide the fact that they were following her, keeping steadily on her tail. But that was probably the point: to show her they were on to her, and to intimidate and harass.

So they knew. But how? Unless Mike had blabbed? Or someone in his entourage? Which would be very unfortunate, since Mike had been the one swearing her to secrecy about their encounter. But if Mike hadn't talked, and she certainly hadn't, then who?

The only explanation was that Mike wasn't the only one being made privy to the news of the sudden windfall that had befallen the Knight clan.

She knew she had to get rid of these people somehow.

She wasn't a stuntwoman, though, and didn't know any nifty tricks on how to shake a tail. So instead she decided to activate the contingency plan she had put in place: to drive straight to the one person she knew who could help her: Odelia Kingsley.

CHAPTER 2

Odelia wasn't an actual detective in the sense that she held a license and took on clients. Nevertheless she still took on the odd case from time to time, since people seemed to believe that she could be instrumental in assisting them in dealing with certain issues they faced. Mostly she tried to steer them in the direction of the police, since she felt they were better suited to deal with the kinds of problems they brought to her. But from time to time someone arrived in her office asking assistance in a matter of the greatest urgency that somehow captured her imagination and her sense of curiosity.

And just such a person was seated in front of her now. Francine Martin was a member of one of Hampton Cove's most prominent families, and as such would have captured the attention of anyone. But the problem she now placed before her was one that she could easily turn into a front-page article. Very unfortunate, therefore, that the first thing Francine insisted on was Odelia's absolute discretion.

"You can't tell anyone," the woman said. "Or talk about it

with anyone. Or write about it in your paper. Is that understood, Mrs. Kingsley?"

Odelia found herself nodding along, even though she knew Dan would never allow her to go off on some wild-goose chase on his dime if there wasn't a big juicy article waiting at the end of the journey.

Francine was a stylish woman about a decade Odelia's senior, but her beauty was marred by a haunted look in her eyes that told Odelia that here sat a woman who was in some serious trouble.

"So what can I do for you, Francine?" she asked.

Francine glanced over her shoulder. "I was followed," she intimated. "All the way into town a car was following me. Which is why I came to you. These people are dangerous, Mrs. Kingsley. I think I managed to fool them. I parked in front of the police station, walked in and immediately out the back. I don't think they followed me in. These are not the kind of people who want to be seen walking into a police station."

"So who are these people, and why are they following you?"

"I'm not sure, but what I do know is that it's all connected to a discovery I made recently. A discovery that turned my life upside down, and my family's life. If I tell you, do you promise not to tell anyone?"

"Of course," said Odelia. "Absolutely."

"My grandmother recently passed away. And on her deathbed she revealed to me that my great-grandfather had a second family. I never knew my great-grandfather, but according to my grandmother the man led a double life for years. Until he left us. I'd known for years that there was some big scandal in the family, but I didn't know the extent until Gran told me. Turns out the man my grandmother knew as Jack Cooper was also known as Ebenezer Knight, Mike Knight's great-grandfather."

Odelia sat back. "I know Mike Knight," she said. "Well, at least vaguely. I interviewed him and his dad once about the old potash mine the Knight family owns and used to operate."

Francine nodded. "That's what this is all about. That old potash mine. Ebenezer—or Jack Cooper as he was known to our side of the family—bought that land shortly after the Second World War. Mining operations started in 1954 and continued for the next thirty years, contributing to the Knight family fortune. The mine closed in the eighties, when they thought they'd profitably extracted everything it held, and the land has sat empty since then. There were plans to develop it but nothing ever came of it."

"Yeah, some conflict with the planning commission," said Odelia.

"Something like that. I don't know the details. Anyway, it's probably a good thing they never got to build an industrial site or a housing estate or whatever, because from what my grandmother revealed to me, there's actual a rich vein of lithium in the ground that was never discovered or exploited."

"Lithium? In Hampton Cove?" Now this was news. Big news.

Francine took a deep breath. "Part of my grandmother's legacy was a diary belonging to Ebenezer Knight. In it he mentions the discovery of lithium and he even drew a map pinpointing its exact location. Back in those days lithium wasn't on anybody's radar, and the discovery wasn't mentioned. I talked to Mike and he was as surprised as I was that there would be lithium in the ground. But if Ebenezer found it, it must be there. And as we both know, lithium is the new gold."

"I'll say it is. With electric cars taking over from cars powered by the internal combustion engine, the industry is going to need all the lithium it can get."

"I know, right? When I told Mike I could tell he got very excited."

"So you talked to your cousin—your distant cousin. So what's going to happen now?"

"Well, that's the problem we're faced with right now," said Francine. "We're sitting on a goldmine here, but we didn't know that until very recently—or at least until I discovered my great-grandfather's diary. So now experts will have to be brought in to determine how rich this seam actually is. And then investments will have to be made to reopen the mine and start operations again."

"That all sounds very exciting," said Odelia with a smile.

"It is. Only…" She bit her lip. "I'm not sure Mike has been entirely honest with me."

"What do you mean?"

"Honestly? I have a hunch that his family has made deals to develop that land, in spite of the planning commission's embargo on any redevelopment plans. I think Mike has already signed a preliminary deal with a real estate developer and he'll have to find a way to get out of it."

"But if this developer discovers that there's lithium in the ground…"

"He won't allow Mike's family to back out. And I have a feeling they have found out. I don't know how, and I don't know who told them, but clearly these people are very interested to know where exactly this lithium deposit is located, and they'll go to extreme lengths to protect their investment."

"And you think these are the people who were following you?"

Francine shook her head. "I'm not sure. But I think so, yes."

"Who else did you tell about the lithium?"

"Only my cousin Mike. And I'm absolutely convinced he wouldn't tell anyone. It's in his best interest to keep a lid on this, since he'll want to get this deal terminated. Mike is a dedicated family man, and he knows this lithium will be his family's saving grace. His financial fortunes haven't been great lately."

"They haven't? But I thought the Knights were extremely wealthy?"

"They used to be," said Francine with a grimace. "I don't know the details, but from what I've been told there have been some bad investments made and the family lost a lot of money over the years."

"So they need that mine."

"They need that mine," Francine confirmed.

"So what are you going to do now?"

"I just had a meeting with Mike, and I told him about the diary. And even though officially I wasn't informed, he'll have to reverse the sale. Without letting on what the real reason is, of course. If he succeeds, he'll be able to hang on to his property—our property. If not..."

"Then Mike will have made this developer very happy indeed," said Odelia, nodding. "I still don't see why you need my help, though, Francine. If your cousin succeeds in getting that deal terminated, then fine. And if not, you should probably talk to a lawyer, not a reporter."

"You don't know the kind of people we're dealing with here, Odelia. The lengths they will go to to get what they want. To be honest with you, I don't think my life or that of my cousin is safe right now. I don't know how much they know or suspect, but I have to believe they know about the lithium.

Which means they'll go to any lengths to protect their investment and make sure they get their hands on that land. And they'll do anything to make sure we don't get in their way."

"But don't they own the land legally at this point?"

"Like I said, I don't know the details, since I wasn't involved in the negotiations, and Mike doesn't even know I know, but I'm sure certain stipulations were made when the contract was signed. They bought the land under the condition they'd build houses. If they decide to turn it into a lithium mine instead…"

"They have no right to do that?"

"I don't think so. But I'm not a lawyer so I don't know."

"They'll try to hang on to that land by any means possible."

"That's what I'm afraid of. And I don't think they're prepared to pay the correct price, based on its true value. They're going to use every dirty trick in the book to get Mike to honor their original deal."

Odelia gave the woman a look of concern. Her heart went out to Francine, and her family. But she still didn't see what she could do. She had no legal experience, nor did she want to end up being involved in some protracted legal wrangling between these two parties. "So…"

"So what I wanted to ask you," said Francine, taking a deep breath. "Is if somehow you can provide me with some form of protection." When Odelia started to protest, she quickly added, "I know you're not a bodyguard, Odelia. And frankly I don't want one. What I had in mind was to simply lie low for a while. Disappear, you know. If they don't know where to find me, I'll be safe."

Odelia shook her head. "I'm not sure…"

"Just until Mike has managed to take care of things. I'm sure it won't be long. He's very clever, and also very professional."

"How long do you think you'd need to be out of circulation?"

"Just a couple of days—two weeks, tops." Francine was directing a pleading look at her that was hard to ignore. "Please?" she said. "I don't know anyone in Hampton Cove, Odelia. And I want to be here when Mike concludes our deal. He's going to pay me a lump sum for the diary, and we'll sign a contract for the exploitation of the mine once all the legal hurdles are cleared. I can't stay at a hotel, since I'm afraid of what will happen once these people realize what's going on. And if I stay with you they won't be able to find me, since we're not related and we don't have any previous connection whatsoever."

Odelia thought for a moment. This was all highly irregular. Though it wasn't the first time she had provided room and board to a person under duress. Or actually on more than one occasion. Once was a retired fitness star, whose life had been in jeopardy. And another time the former prime minister of the United Kingdom, after he'd been forced to flee the country when his popularity had dropped precipitously following some scandal. Neither experience had been a particularly enjoyable one, to be honest. But she couldn't very well say no to Francine. The woman was clearly terrified of what might happen to her.

"All right," she finally said. "You can stay with us. But on one condition and one condition only."

"Name it," said Francine, visibly relieved.

"No one can know where you are. If they did, not only your safety would be jeopardized, but also the safety of my family, you understand."

"Absolutely," said Francine. "Oh, Odelia, thank you so much!"

"You're very welcome," said Odelia warmly.

CHAPTER 3

Dooley had been sniffing here and there and wondering what this strange specimen could possibly be. He'd never seen anything like it, not even on the Discovery Channel, as everyone knows a prime source of both entertainment and information. The creature hadn't stirred since Dooley had made its discovery on the lawn behind the house. It sat on top of a small mound of freshly dug soil and looked like a rat, only smaller. Though it could have been a mouse, of course, only bigger. Hard to know for sure!

It had a tiny head with a protruding nose. It had no ears he could see and brown fur. It had very large digits on its front paws, and plenty of whiskers surrounding its long pink nose. Dooley couldn't see its eyes, but he was sure it must have them. All creatures had eyes, right? How else could they move around?

Max, his best friend and housemate, could have provided some illumination as to the mysterious creature's nature, but unfortunately Max had returned indoors for a much-needed bathroom break.

Harriet and Brutus were also absent from the scene, and so it was up to Dooley to a) determine the nature of this strange beast; b) determine whether it formed a clear and present danger to Dooley's home and its residents; and c) whether possible countermeasures should be instigated to make sure the threat—if there was a threat—could be eradicated.

And that's when the creature stirred!

Dooley jumped about a foot in the air, and quickly hid behind a nearby bush containing about half a dozen roses. In his haste to take cover he must have nudged one of them, for the rose now decided to make the great leap into the beyond and dropped down to provide some welcome mulch for present and future generations of the common earthworm and other denizens of the undersoil.

The creature, which shall remain nameless for the present because no classification seemed applicable, now opened its eyes—it did indeed have them!—and gazed at Dooley with a curious expression.

"Hey there," said the creature, a grating sound to Dooley's strained ears. "I'm Jackie. Who are you?"

"Um… Smith Jones," said Dooley, figuring he better provide a fake name, just in case the creature turned out to be some kind of monster ready to devour him whole.

"Hi, Smith Jones," said Jackie, then stretched. "Now that was a glorious nap." She glanced around, smacking her lips for some reason, as if she had just enjoyed a copious meal. "Where am I, by the way? I arrived overnight, and as we all know traveling in the dark provides one with a set of obstacles, such as there are: not being fully aware of one's exact surroundings."

"You're in… Cleveland," Dooley said, figuring he might as well give a fake location, just in case the creature was the vanguard of an enemy force ready to attack.

"Cleveland?" said Jackie with a frown. "That's odd. I could have sworn I was in the Hamptons." But then she shrugged. "I guess I was mistaken."

"So… what are you, exactly?" asked Dooley, still eyeing the creature closely, just in case it made any sudden moves causing him to beat a strategic retreat and go hide in the basement.

Jackie grinned. "A lady never tells, Smith Jones," she said. "Hasn't anyone ever told you that?"

"Told me what?" asked Dooley, confused by this curious statement.

"Anything! Her age, her proclivities…."

"What's a pro… a prog… a procklimity?"

Jackie eyed him strangely. "If I didn't know any better I'd say you're still a kitten, Smith Jones, but your body structure appears to belie that classification. So what can I do for you at this juncture?"

"Do for me? What do you mean, do for me?" asked Dooley, thinking this situation was becoming more and more fraught with a distinct aspect of weirdness.

"Well, I am here to fulfill all of your wishes," said Jackie cheerfully. "So what is it you want today, Smith Jones? And remember, three wishes is all you get, not four, not five—just three. So use them wisely."

He stared at the creature. He'd heard of this type of thing, where some genie suddenly appeared from a bottle, like smoke wafting from a candle, and sort of materialized out of thin air and started granting wishes to all and sundry. Could this be such a genie? It didn't look like a genie, of course. But then again he'd never actually been face to face with a genie before, so what did he know what genies looked like in the wild? "Um…" he said, thinking hard. What did he want? Tough question! But then he got it. "I wish for all of my friends and all of my humans to be healthy and happy forever and ever."

Jackie gave him a strange look. "That's very noble of you, Smith Jones. Very noble indeed. But I'm afraid that's one particular wish I simply cannot grant you."

"Oh, but why?" he asked.

"Since it concerns others. The only type of wishes I can grant you are the ones that benefit yourself. So what shall it be, young man? And like I said, wish wisely. And limit your wishes to three only."

"Um..." Now this was even harder. A wish that only benefited himself? After thinking this through for a little while longer, the creature staring at him with glittering eyes and her head cocked to one side, he finally had to admit defeat. "I don't know, Jackie," he said sadly. "I don't really have any wishes for myself alone. Everything I can think of is connected to my friends or the humans who take care of us."

Jackie smiled. "You're not like most creatures I meet, Smith Jones. No wishes of your own, eh? Curiouser and curiouser. Then again, I may have been pulling your paw here, young Padawan."

He glanced down at his paw, and when he saw that no pulling action was taking place, he frowned. "I don't understand," he admitted.

"I'm not a genie, you silly! Genies don't actually exist. I'm just a mole."

"A mole? You mean like a mole for the enemy?" he asked, moving a little further back even more.

This time Jackie laughed a hearty laugh. "A mole for the enemy indeed. No, I'm an actual mole, Smith Jones. The kind that digs holes in people's backyards? Don't tell me you've never met a mole before."

"No, I haven't," Dooley confessed honestly. "So what do you do, Jackie, apart from digging holes?"

"Oh, I snap up the odd morsel of food from time to time," said Jackie. "And generally I try and make sure my survival is guaranteed and also that of my offspring."

"Your… offspring?" he asked, glancing left and right. So there were more of these 'moles' around? Maybe an entire expeditionary 'mole' force? This was worse than he thought!

"Yeah, you may be happy to know that my husband Dave is preparing a nice cozy burrow right now. But I just had to pop out for a bit of fresh air, you know. Not healthy to stay underground all the time."

"Uh-huh?" said Dooley, glancing at the ground beneath his paws, and fully expecting it to start moving any moment now, an entire army of these so-called moles suddenly rising up and taking him prisoner.

"Okay, well, it was sure great making your acquaintance, Smith Jones. But I have to run. Can't leave the old hubby preparing that nest all by himself, now can I? That wouldn't be very nice of me, would it now?"

"No, I guess not," said Dooley, still watching the ground for signs of movement.

"Okay, so see you around," said Jackie, and when he looked up, he saw she was gone.

He blinked. "Jackie?"

But there was no response. As suddenly as she had appeared, she had disappeared, possibly to join her husband, who might or might not be the general of an invading army ready to take over Hampton Cove!

When Max came ambling out of the house five minutes later, looking as happy as any cat can be after having made delivery of a nice big poo, he found his friend Dooley looking extremely agitated.

"Max, we're under attack!" the fluffy Ragamuffin announced.

"Under attack?" asked Max. "What do you mean?"

But Dooley had no time to go into detail, as he had taken to shaking like a leaf. All he was ready to divulge at this point was that, "I saw the face of the enemy, Max. And it was terrifying!"

CHAPTER 4

I stared at Dooley with some astonishment. "Alien invaders? What are you talking about?"

"I saw them, Max!" said my friend, and I could see he was much disconcerted, judging from the way he was quaking where he stood. "I saw one of them," he corrected himself. "But she accidentally let slip that there are more, and they're gathering right beneath our paws as we speak—getting ready to invade!"

Involuntarily my eyes dropped to the ground, and so did Dooley's, and it was a testament to his conviction that I was starting to wonder if some alien invasion force was actually gathering strength underneath the nicely manicured lawn of our humans Odelia and Chase Kingsley. Hitherto I'd known of worms and other bugs creating a living for themselves in the bowels of the earth, and maybe even more exotic creatures when you dug a little deeper. But an alien army? That seemed a little farfetched to me.

"So what did she look like, this alien?" I asked.

"She was brown," said Dooley, nodding as he recollected the salient details of this auspicious meeting with an alien.

"With shiny velvety fur, a pointy pink nose, whiskers, and weird little eyes that were practically invisible. And something I noticed was that she had very big feet for such a small creature."

"And what did she tell you, exactly?" I prodded.

"Well, first she said she was a genie and that I could do three wishes. But then when it turned out I didn't have three wishes, she laughed and said she was pulling my paw and she wasn't a genie but a mole."

"A mole!" I said, laughing. "You met a mole?"

"I did," Dooley confirmed. "And then she said she had to leave because her husband Dave was preparing their burrow. And then when I looked, she was gone. Poof! Vanished into thin air!"

"Vanished into a freshly dug tunnel, you mean."

"You think so?" said Dooley, eyes wide.

"Of course. That's what moles do, Dooley. They dig tunnels and create burrows where they live. Some people think they're annoying, since they make a mess of your yard, but they're very useful creatures."

"I think it's all very ominous, Max. Very ominous and suspicious. But I told her she was in Cleveland, and that my name was Smith Jones so that should throw them off the scent, wouldn't you say?"

"Oh, I'll bet it will throw her off the scent," I said with a smile. Even though my human's husband Chase and her dad Tex probably wouldn't agree with me, the disaster had been averted. Both men love their backyard, and like pottering in it when they have some time to spare. And since moles aren't exactly the avid gardener's best friend, they wouldn't be hanging out the welcome flag for the tiny creatures.

"I don't think we have anything to worry about, buddy," I told my friend. "Moles aren't aliens. They're creatures just like you and me. Only instead of living in people's homes, they like to live underground."

"Oh," said Dooley, much sobered by this piece of information. "So... they're not the vanguard of an alien invasion?"

"There's nothing alien about moles," I assured him. "They may look different, and they probably are different, but they didn't arrive here from another planet, and they're not out to colonize our world."

"Okay," said Dooley, as he processed this. "So... I did tell her my name was Smith Jones, Max, and that we're in Cleveland."

"So?"

"So I lied to her, Max. And lying is a bad thing, right?"

"You lied for a good cause," I assured him. "You lied because you thought she was up to all kinds of bad stuff. But now that you know she's not, next time you see her you can set the record straight."

"I will," he said fervently. "She did seem nice, but then you know what alien invaders are like: they're all very charming and sweet, until they suddenly bite your head off and zap you with their laser beam."

"Since I've never met an alien invader, I couldn't say, Dooley."

"What's all this about an alien invasion?" asked Brutus, who had joined us. The big black cat had gone for a stroll around the block, and now positioned himself on the lawn, preparatory to taking a load off his paws.

"Dooley met a mole, and somehow he became convinced she was part of the vanguard for an alien invasion force," I explained.

"Oh, Dooley," said Brutus with a slight grin. "You're too funny."

Harriet also joined us. The white Persian seemed tired, and as she lay down next to her mate, her eyes drooped closed. Within seconds she was fast asleep, and we hadn't even heard the sound of her voice yet.

"What's wrong with her?" I asked therefore.

Brutus grimaced. "I think she ate something," he intimated. "Hasn't been feeling well all morning."

"Must be a bad prawn," said Dooley decidedly. "I heard Chase tell Odelia this morning that he ate a bad prawn yesterday, and he felt as if he was going to die. This was after he got back from the gym, though, so I'm not sure if it's the prawn that made him feel like he was about to die or the gym."

Brutus and I exchanged a look of worry. Words to the effect that one of our humans is on the verge of a fatal collapse never cease to worry me to some extent. We are wholly dependent on our humans, after all. And if one of them were to suddenly shuffle off this mortal coil, it wouldn't bode well for any of us.

"So how is he?" asked Brutus.

"Oh, I'm sure he's fine," said Dooley. "Prawns are tough, Brutus. They're survivors."

"Not the prawn, silly," said Brutus. "Chase."

"I don't know," said Dooley. "All I know is that he didn't go to work this morning. He got up, went to the gym, then came home again and said he was going straight to bed because he wasn't feeling well."

We all glanced up at the house. "So… he's home right now?" I asked.

"Oh, sure," said Dooley. "He's upstairs in bed, resting."

"But did they at least call a doctor?" asked Brutus.

"I'll bet they did," said Dooley, though he didn't sound entirely convinced.

Our human's dad is a doctor, you see, so it's easy to call a doctor, since he lives right next door.

"I'll bet Tex took a good look at Chase before he left for

work this morning," I said, trying to convince both myself and the others that everything was fine. But try as I might, the specter of Chase being sick like a dog and ailing wouldn't leave me.

And so we decided to go and see for ourselves if the stalwart cop was all right.

Brutus gave Harriet a gentle nudge, and when the latter woke up, he explained to her that Chase was possibly on the precipice of death, and that woke her up immediately.

"We have to save him!" she said, as she followed us through the pet flap. "If Chase dies, Odelia will be devastated. And we all know what happens when humans are depressed. They stop caring for themselves and for anyone else as well. So she'll probably get rid of us so she can focus on her recovery from such a big shock."

And so it was with a touch of alarm that we set paw for the upstairs landing, and then immediately headed in the direction of the master bedroom, where we hoped to find a sign of life, but feared we might be too late instead.

We jumped on the bed as one cat, and homed in on Chase, who was indeed in bed, and not, as was his habit, chasing criminals or generally being in the service of the local population as a police officer.

We gathered around the man's head, and stared down at him. Dooley was positioned near his forehead, I covered his left ear, Harriet his right ear, and Brutus had taken up position on top of his chest.

"He doesn't look good," Harriet determined.

"He's sweating," Dooley said.

"He's very pale," I added my voice to the conversation.

"I think he's dead," said Brutus somberly.

"I don't think so," said Harriet. "You're moving up and down, smoochie poo. And that means his lungs are still pumping oxygen."

"Oh, right," said Brutus as he became aware of this strange fact.

He was indeed moving up and down at regular intervals, which was an uplifting sign, to be honest. Dead humans don't have that effect on us, after all.

"But then why is he looking so pale and why is he sweating so much?" asked Dooley. Then his eyes went wide. "You guys! He's probably dead but he doesn't know it yet! Quick, Max, do CPR!"

"I can't do CPR," I told him. "My paws are too small." And besides, I didn't feel comfortable putting my lips on those of our human. For one thing, Chase had bad breath—possibly from the consumption of that bad prawn. And secondly, his face was wet with sweat. It all felt very icky to me, to be honest.

"If we don't do something, he will die!" said Dooley. He now raised his eyes heavenward. "Oh, I wish now I'd known this sooner. I could have used this as one of my three wishes."

"What wishes?" asked Brutus. "What are you talking about?"

"I met an alien genie this morning. And she granted me three wishes. But then she also said I couldn't use any of my wishes for others—so that wouldn't have done Chase any good either," he said as he thought this thing through. "And besides, she wasn't an alien genie after all. Max says she's a mole, and moles can't grant wishes. Or can they?" He directed a hopeful look at me, but I merely shook my head, and he deflated somewhat, placing a paw on Chase's brow, possibly to take his temperature.

"Okay, so we should probably call a doctor," I said. "It's clear that he's in a pretty bad way, and if we don't get help in here soon, he might die."

And so it was decided, after some verbal wrangling, that Brutus and I would fetch Tex, while Dooley and Harriet stayed with Chase, making sure he didn't collapse and die on us, as humans seem prone to do on occasion.

Soon Brutus and I were on our way to warn Odelia's dad that the life of his beloved son-in-law was in mortal danger.

We put some pep in our step as we made our way to the doctor's office, which is located not all that far from where we live. The problem on these occasions is always that it's imperative to impress a sense of urgency upon the person you're talking to, and secondly trying to convey a message to any human who isn't Odelia or her mom or grandma is always a difficult proposition. Lucky for us Gran was at the reception desk, and so the moment we strode in, Brutus announced, "Chase is dying, Gran. You have to tell Tex to go save his life."

I'd never seen Gran react with such alacrity as she did at that very moment. "Dying!" she cried, rocketing up from her chair. Lucky for us there was no one in the waiting room, or they would have been extremely surprised to see this old lady discussing these matters of life and death with a pair of cats.

"Yeah, he's pale and sweaty and he didn't respond when we tried to wake him up," I explained.

"There's one thing we didn't think of, Max," said Brutus. "We should have tried acupuncture. Humans typically respond well to the treatment."

It was true. The moment we put our claws into a human's flesh, they usually respond with a great measure of alarm. It wakes them right up, and puts the roses back in their cheeks.

Gran had already disappeared into the inner office, which is where Tex holds court, and reappeared with the doctor in tow. Tex was grabbing his doctor's bag, and was ready to save lives—that of his son-in-law in particular.

"Where is he?!" he demanded, glancing around the

waiting room. We could see he was much stirred by this piece of news we had come to impart.

"Home," I said. "He's laid up in bed and I don't think he's got much longer to live."

"He ate a bad prawn," said Brutus sadly. "There should probably be a law against prawns, considering the lives they claim every year. Charles Manson is nothing compared to these miniature mass murderers."

"But I checked him this morning," said Tex, after Gran had translated our words. "And he was fine."

"And now he's unresponsive," I said. "So we better hurry. He might not have a lot longer to live."

Tex only needed to be told once, and then we were all piling into the doctor's car, and he took off like a bat out of hell. It wasn't a long trip, and before long he parked in front of the house and we all hurried out.

Gran opened the front door—she has her own key—and we stormed up the stairs, Tex first, Gran a close second, and Brutus and I bringing up the rear.

In the bedroom, a bad odor seemed to pervade the air, hanging like a miasma in the small room. It was the reek of death, I knew, and I was already envisioning a future for us without Chase. It would be hard, not least for Grace, his little girl, who had barely known her father and now already he would be taken away from her. Cut down in his prime, as they say.

Tex immediately plunked his doctor's bag on the floor and bent over the ailing patient. He placed a hand on his brow, opened his eyes to see if there was still life left in the man, checked his pulse, and finally stepped back with a sigh. "Heart rate slow, skin pale, pupils constricted," he murmured. "No fever..."

"Is he going to live, Tex?" Gran demanded. The old lady was wringing her hands, prey to a welter of emotion.

"Of course he's going to live," Tex snapped, though he looked both nervous and thoughtful.

"That prawn has a lot to answer for," Brutus reiterated his earlier sentiment about the pernicious species.

Just then, the front door slammed, and we all looked up in alarm. Moments later there was a heavy footfall on the stairs, and before long Odelia stepped into the room, looking very surprised.

"What's going on?" she asked. "What are you all doing here?"

"It's Chase," said Gran. "We're afraid he's not well, honey."

"What do you mean?" said Odelia, and immediately hurried to her husband's side. After she had reassured herself that he was still breathing and that his heart was still beating, she turned to her dad. "I gave him that sleeping pill this morning, Dad. Is he having a bad reaction?"

Tex blinked, as if coming out of a stupor. "Sleeping pill?"

"Yeah, you told me he needed to rest, after he'd been up half the night puking his guts out. Then this morning he felt better so he went to the gym, even though I told him not to. But then he started feeling drowsy so he came home and went straight to bed. So I gave him half a sleeping pill so he could sleep it off."

Tex smiled uncertainly. "I-I forgot about that."

"So is that why he isn't responding?" asked Gran, giving her son-in-law a look of suspicion.

"That may have something to do with it," Tex confessed.

"Oh, Tex!" said Gran, throwing up her hands. "And here I was already planning his funeral!"

"His *funeral*!" said Odelia, much shocked.

"Yeah, the cats came storming into the office, telling us that Chase was dying," Gran explained. "So naturally when we found him like this we thought the worst."

Odelia gave her dad a critical look. "You didn't give him the wrong pill, did you, Dad?"

"Oh, I'm sure I didn't," said Tex, but all of a sudden he didn't seem so sure of himself anymore. "Do you still have the box?"

Odelia opened the nightstand's drawer and took out a box and handed it to her dad. He studied it, and smiled. "Perfectly innocent," he said. "Just as I suspected. He's simply enjoying a good rest. He'll be right as rain when he wakes up."

"*If* he wakes up," said Dooley, who was still positioned near Chase's head, though by now he was practically on top of his face.

"Can you please not do that, Dooley?" said Odelia.

"Do what?" asked Dooley innocently.

"Lie on top of Chase's face. You're making it hard for him to breathe."

"Oh, right," said Dooley, and removed himself from the man's visage.

"And can you please not sit on his chest, Brutus?" she asked. Brutus, who had assumed his old position, grumbled something but did as he was told. Now the only one who was left was Harriet, who for some reason was breathing hard into Chase's right ear.

"I'm giving him the kiss of life," she explained when Odelia gave her a critical look.

"The kiss of life usually involves planting your lips on top of the lips of the person you're trying to save," Odelia explained patiently. "Not blow into their ear."

"Yeah, it's called mouth-to-mouth for a reason," said Gran. "Not mouth-to-ear, toots."

"Oh, fine," said Harriet, as she got up from her perch near the man's ear. "I was trying to save his life."

Odelia was fussing over Chase, applying a wet washcloth

Gran had brought from the bathroom to his brow, and generally all attention was riveted on the victim of the bad prawn, when suddenly my attention was drawn to a person standing in the doorway.

"Is there anything I can do?" this person asked.

Gran gasped, Tex blew out a breath of surprise, and the cat contingent started hissing at this intruder. Our claws came out, our backs went up and our tails distended to three times their normal size. The newcomer, taking this all in, recoiled in shock.

"It's all right," Odelia hastened to say. "This is Francine Martin. She'll be staying with us for a little while. Francine, please meet my grandmother, my dad and my husband. And these four wild animals are Max, Dooley, Harriet and Brutus. They're the sweetest cats on earth, but right now they seem to have taken leave of their senses. Behave, you guys," she added for our sake. "Be nice to our guest."

"At least she's not a mole," said Dooley as he studied the newcomer more closely. "Though she could still be an alien invader!"

CHAPTER 5

The woman Odelia had introduced as Francine Martin seemed uncomfortable, especially when faced with no less than four cats, an old lady and a middle-aged man grouped around a man who looked as if he might as well be dead.

She was staring in horror and shock at Chase, turning almost as pale as the sick cop, but Odelia quickly disabused her of the notion that her husband might be dead. "He's simply asleep," she explained.

"He ate a bad prawn," Brutus added, though of course the woman didn't understand what he was saying as she didn't belong to the small group of people who can actually talk to cats, like Odelia, her mom and her grandmother.

"I'll show you to your room," Odelia said, and proceeded to lead Francine to the guest room, which seemed appropriate since she was a guest.

And since cats are possibly the most curious creatures on earth, we all followed in their wake.

The guest bedroom isn't much of a guest bedroom at all, since Chase at some point decided that we didn't need guests, and that his physical well-being was much more important than his social life, and transformed the second bedroom into a home gym. Then at some point a desk was added, since everybody needs a home office, and so now this home gym slash home office slash guest bedroom looked a lot more like a home storage space than an actual cozy bedroom in which to welcome a beloved guest.

Francine glanced around and didn't seem entirely impressed by her new surroundings.

"Why doesn't she stay at a hotel?" Dooley suggested.

"Or next door?" Brutus added. "Marge and Tex have plenty of space."

"No, they do not," said Harriet quickly. "Gran would never allow it," she explained.

"You mean you won't allow it," I said. "Since you and Brutus like to sleep at the foot of Marge and Tex's bed, and Dooley likes to sleep at the foot of Gran's bed, so there's no room for anyone else."

"It's a modest family home," Harriet insisted. "If this woman wants comfort she needs to go to a hotel. There are plenty of those around, after all. And they would only be too happy to welcome her and provide her with the comfort and the luxury to which she has grown accustomed."

The woman did look as if she was used to a certain luxury, I had to admit. Her hair was glossy like you sometimes see in those shampoo commercials on television, and she was wearing what I could only assume were some very expensive threads. She was also very pretty, with milky white skin, cornflower blue eyes and a body that wouldn't look out of place on the cover of *Cosmopolitan.*

"Who is she, though?" asked Brutus. "And why is she staying with us?"

"I have no idea," I said. "But I'm sure Odelia will explain to us soon."

Odelia had finished profusely apologizing for the state of the room, and had explained that they didn't often entertain guests.

"It's perfectly all right, Odelia," Francine assured her. "This will do just fine. And besides, it's only for the time being, until Mike figures out what to do about these developers."

"I hope he can work things out," said Odelia fervently. "Are you sure he's safe, though?"

"Oh, I'm sure Mike can take care of himself. And besides, he probably has security."

"Have you told him where you will be staying?"

"No, I think it's best if I don't," said Francine. "I trust him implicitly, of course, but these people managed to find out about the mine somehow, so maybe his phone is being bugged, or my phone, or our cars or homes." She shrugged. "Who knows what these people are capable of? Or to what lengths they're prepared to go to make sure this deal goes through."

"You have to warn him, though."

"I will. I'll tell him to watch his back."

We all shared a look of concern. "Watch his back? People who bug phones or cars or homes?" said Harriet. "This all sounds as if Odelia got herself mixed up in something pretty bad again, you guys."

It did sound exactly like that.

"Maybe Francine is hiding from the mob," Brutus ventured.

"Or maybe she's a witness and Odelia is providing witness protection," Harriet supplied.

"Or maybe she's an alien and she's managed to look like a human," Dooley suggested. "Just like those moles outside!"

"Dooley, those moles are simply that," I said. "Moles. And

this woman is just a woman. There are no alien invaders involved."

"I think I'll feel right at home," said Francine as she sat down on the bed and tested the mattress. She glanced up at Odelia. "I just hope it won't be too much trouble for you or your husband."

"Oh, that's all right," Odelia said. "I'm only happy to help. And if there's anything else I can do for you, just let me know."

Suddenly Francine's eyes turned up, and as she raised a trembling finger at the ceiling she started screaming her head off. We all looked, and saw that she was pointing at Grover, the large spider who had recently selected our house as his new home and had decided to become a permanent fixture there.

"Kill it!" Francine screamed. "Kill it dead!"

"That's Grover," Odelia said, using her most soothing voice. "He's not poisonous. Doesn't bite or anything."

"It's a monster!" She had gotten up from the bed as if stung. "I'm sorry, Odelia, but I hate spiders. Maybe this was a bad idea after all."

"Okay, so maybe you'll take our room," Odelia suggested, thinking on her feet as is her habit. "And Chase and I will take this room for now. How about that? And of course we'll make sure Grover doesn't come anywhere near you."

Francine, whose lips were still trembling, nodded anxiously. "Fine. That's fine."

"Okay, that's settled then," said Odelia with a determined nod of the head. "Chase and I will move in here…" She eyed the narrow single bed with a touch of concern. "And you'll take the main bedroom."

This would all have been swell, if Francine hadn't suddenly started screaming again. This time she was pointing at the four of us. She placed a hand on her heart. "Those cats. They're following me!"

"They're just curious, that's all," Odelia assured her. Then she gave Francine a look of concern. "You're not allergic, are you?"

Francine shook her head. "I'm not fond of cats, that's for sure. But no, as far as I know I'm not allergic."

"Thank God," I said. "Imagine if we had to move into this small room along with Odelia and Chase and not come anywhere near Francine from now on."

"But can you keep them away from me?" Francine asked. "It's just that… being in the state that I am, my nerves are shattered as it is, so…"

"Of course," said Odelia. "I'll make sure the cats don't come anywhere near you from now on." She gave us a stern-faced look. "Is that understood? Stay away from Francine, you hear? Leave her be."

"Yes, Odelia," we all said dutifully.

But I can tell you that we weren't happy about it. Not happy at all!

CHAPTER 6

Dooley wasn't very pleased with the situation, but what could he do? It now seemed as if they were under attack from every side: outside an army of alien moles was gathering, getting ready to take over the planet one small town at a time, and inside the house they had been forbidden from coming anywhere near Francine, who had taken over the best room in the house, and seemed determined to stay there indefinitely. And then of course there was Chase, who was probably a lot worse than Tex had convinced Odelia he was. So very soon now they would be kicked out of the house, because of Francine, and possibly kicked out of their backyard, because of the mole invasion.

No, things were looking bad. Very bad indeed! And the worst part was that Max didn't seem convinced of this obvious fact. On the contrary. He kept saying that everything would be just fine, and that things would work out—nothing to worry about at all!

Dooley had once read that sometimes even the greatest minds suffered from these kinds of delusions. And clearly Max was suffering from exactly such a delusion now. Things were going from bad to worse, but Max simply refused to accept that it was so.

I have to convince him, Dooley thought. I have to make Max see that something needs to be done!

But how? And then he had it. He would simply have to organize a meeting of these two great opposite forces: the aliens on the one hand, and Max on the other. That way Max could convince himself that the threat was real, and his big brain would start working on a solution. Because as long as he didn't appreciate the danger they were in, he would remain complacent… until it was too late!

The meeting in the guest bedroom was over, and Francine had been introduced to the main bedroom, where Gran and Tex and Odelia were engaged in the major undertaking of trying to move Chase from this bed to the much smaller bed in the guest bedroom. To move a person is hard enough as it is, but to move a person who doesn't cooperate is even harder.

"Dead weight," Gran grumbled at a certain point.

"Did you just call my husband dead weight, Gran?" asked Odelia sternly.

"No, I did not," Gran assured her. "I was just pointing out that his head weighs a lot, and that's probably because he's so very clever."

"Mh," said Odelia.

Finally they managed to move the patient to the second bedroom, and tuck him safely into bed.

Odelia touched the cheek of her sleeping husband, a look of concern on her own face. "Are you sure he's all right, Dad? It's just that he looks awfully pale to me."

"Oh, he's absolutely fine," Tex assured her. "When he wakes up he'll be right as rain."

But the look on his face when he glanced down at his patient spoke volumes: he wasn't all that sure at all!

I'd seen that look, and Dooley had, too. In fact all four of us had seen it, and we shared a look of concern of our own.

"I don't think Tex is telling Odelia everything," said Harriet.

"No, I don't think so either," said Brutus.

"I knew it!" said Dooley. "He's dying and Tex doesn't want to admit it!"

"I don't think he's dying," I said. "But he's probably in a much worse way than Tex is letting on."

"But why would he lie about that?" asked Harriet. "Wouldn't it be more prudent to take him to a hospital if he's really in such a bad way?"

"Maybe he gave him the wrong pill," Brutus suggested. "And now he's afraid someone will find out and he will lose his license to practice medicine."

It was possible, of course. But on the other hand, Tex is very fond of his son-in-law, and I couldn't imagine him doing anything to hurt the man.

But then Odelia ushered us all out, and suggested in no uncertain terms that we better go and stay with her parents for the time being, considering Francine's cat allergy that wasn't really an allergy, but sounded very much like an allergy to me.

Once outside, we gathered in the backyard, in our usual spot on the patio. "We're being kicked out of the house, you guys," Brutus said sadly. "Can you believe it? Kicked out of our own home by our very own human!"

"That's certainly what it looks like to me," I agreed.

"At least we still have Marge and Tex's place," said Harriet. "Imagine if we got kicked out of there as well."

It was a thought that didn't bear contemplating. We were down from two homes to just the one. Which didn't bode well for the future, I had to admit.

Just then the ground seemed to move in our immediate

vicinity, and Dooley shrieked. "It's the aliens! They're starting their attack! Save yourselves!"

But before he could streak off like a headless chicken, I placed a paw on his shoulder. "How many times do I have to tell you, Dooley? It's just moles. They don't cause any problem to anyone."

"Except to someone like Tex, who likes to keep his backyard nice and pristine," Brutus pointed out.

But Tex had other things on his mind, for as he walked out of the house, his hands deeply shoved into his pockets, he was looking at the ground, a big frown on his face. He took one look at the shifting earth, and at the furry little face that briefly surfaced, its nose twitching and then burrowing down again, and walked on.

He hadn't even noticed the mole, much less worried about its arrival in our midst.

Tex walked away, soon followed by Gran, and disappeared through the opening in the hedge between our backyard and his own. We all stared after him with a look of concern. It wasn't like Tex to look so frowny-faced. Something was going on, and so I vowed to get to the bottom of this thing.

But before we could discuss a possible plan of campaign, Francine had walked out of the house, took a good look at us, her face contorted into a look of distaste, and bellowed, "Odelia! Those cats are here again and they're staring at me in a very threatening manner!"

Odelia quickly came out of the house, saw us, and clapped her hands. "Shoo," she said. "I told you to stay away from Francine, didn't I? So shoo, you guys—shoo!"

And so shoo we did. But we did so under protest. Oh, yes, we did.

CHAPTER 7

If Max and his friends thought Jackie had popped up for no particular reason except to show her pretty face, they were very much mistaken. Because Jackie wasn't like other moles. She was a mole with a social conscience. A mole who deeply cared about the people in whose garden she made her home. And to say she worried about what she had observed so far of the residence where she was a guest would be an understatement. She had watched and she had listened from her unique vantage point three feet deep, and each time she popped her head up she had noticed that things weren't well in the household that identified itself as the Kingsleys. The lady of the house seemed unusually preoccupied with the fate that had been bestowed upon her husband, a man answering to the name Chase. And the cats that lived in that house didn't look very happy either, especially now that a new guest had arrived in their midst, a guest who looked like she was intending to stay there for an indefinite period of time.

Francine Martin might look like the girl next door, but from long experience Jackie knew that these so-called girls next door were rarely that. Quite the contrary, in fact. And as she worried and thought about the things she'd overheard, she confided in her husband, "I don't think things are going well above ground, Dave."

"Oh? And why is that?" asked Dave, who was an unusually attentive husband—a husband who, unlike most husbands, actually listened to his wife when she had something to say.

"That Odelia person has just kicked out her cats, and all because some guest that's come to stay has declared she doesn't like them hanging around. Imagine if she told Odelia she doesn't like moles. Is she going to demand that she kick us out, too?"

"I very much doubt that, sweetheart," said Dave with a smile as he put the finishing touches to the burrow they had dug and declared their new home away from home. "Humans rarely bother with moles, unless we make too much of a mess, of course. In which case they might turn nasty. But as long as we go about our business in an inconspicuous way, this new guest shouldn't pose any problem to us."

"I wouldn't be too sure of that," said Jackie with a pensive frown. "First she kicked out the cats, then she made a stink about some spider who seems to have taken up residence in their home, and I'm sure next thing we know she'll start complaining about some other permanent resident she wants permanently dislodged. I know people like this Francine person, Dave, and I'm telling you that girl is trouble."

"Well, it's no concern of ours, sweetie," said Dave as he sat back and studied the bed he had made from compressed earth. It looked very sturdy and very comfy indeed, and it wasn't that Jackie wasn't grateful. She was. Very much so. But right now she had other things on her mind than their nice new bed.

"I know it's no concern of ours," she said. So why bother sticking her twitchy little nose in? She had no idea. She just knew she had to do something. It was the mother hen side of her personality. Her own mother was exactly the same: always getting involved in things that shouldn't concern her.

"I'll start on the kitchen next, shall I?" said Dave.

"I'm just going to pop up for a moment," she said in response. "I met this nice cat this morning named Smith Jones who told me we're in Cleveland."

Dave stared at her. "We're not in Cleveland, sweetie. We're in the Hamptons."

"Oh, I know that, and I also know that his name isn't really Smith Jones. But he's such a well-behaved young cat, with such good manners, and we got along so great that I think I'll pay him another visit. Maybe there's something I can do to get him through this difficult time he's facing right now."

"And I say you should probably mind your own business," said Dave with a touch of severity. He might be the best husband a girl could ever wish for, but he had a habit of throwing his weight about when he thought he was right and she was wrong.

"Of course, Dave," she said. "You're absolutely right. I shouldn't poke my nose into stuff that doesn't concern me."

"Now you're talking," said Dave. "So what do you think, sweetie? Do the kitchen next? We have to put those worms I caught somewhere, especially after I bit their heads off so they wouldn't go anywhere."

"Absolutely," she said. "You go start on that kitchen, honey. Make it nice and big."

"Will do," said Dave happily.

And so while Dave got busy installing a new kitchen, she decided to pop up and see what was what. She might have promised her husband she wouldn't butt in, but then she wasn't going to tell him what she was up to, now was she?

Through long association with Dave she had become convinced that the best way to maintain peace and harmony at home was not to divulge her every thought to him. What he didn't know, he couldn't get worried about.

Traversing one of a maze of tunnels they had dug in their eternal search for grub, she emerged from the underground and saw to her surprise that no cats were around, not even that nice Dooley, as she had heard the other cats call him. The only thing she could detect was a large bird trying to extract a worm from the lawn. She frowned in dismay. "Excuse me!" she yelled. "That worm is mine!"

The bird didn't pay her any mind, though. Instead, it finished extracting the worm from its hiding place, and took flight.

Jackie shook her head. What is the world coming to, she thought, if birds started stealing her food? But at least it hadn't eaten her, which would have been even worse. She popped out of the hole and tripped across the lawn in search of her new friend. She finally found him in the next backyard, and whispered, "Pssst!"

Dooley slowly turned his head away from his friends, with whom he had been deep in conversation about a topic that didn't concern her.

"Psssst!" she repeated, trying to attract his attention.

Finally Dooley decided to give her his full attention. "What do you want?" he asked, and for some reason he looked more than a little nervous.

"I want you to know that I'll be keeping an eye on that new guest of yours," she told him. "It's not right what she's doing, young Smith Jones. She can't just kick you out of your own home like that."

Dooley merely stared at her, but didn't respond. At which

point a large cat approached, and studied her with a kindly eye.

She recoiled a little, thinking this cat was way too big for comfort. Until now she had only seen Dooley's friends from a distance, and since a mole's eyesight is notoriously bad she hadn't taken into account how big this specimen was. This cat was huge!

"Hi," said the cat. "My name is Max and I'm a friend of Dooley's."

"Surely you mean Smith Jones?" she asked.

"Absolutely," said Max with a wink. "Smith Jones. Also known as Dooley."

"Max!" said Smith Jones-slash-Dooley. "You shouldn't have told Jackie my real name!"

"Dooley thinks you're an alien invader," Max explained. "Now we both know that you're not an alien invader but that you are in actual fact a mole. But Dooley doesn't seem to be able to get that into his nut. So please tell him yourself that you haven't arrived from another galaxy to conquer and invade, will you?"

Jackie grinned. She already liked this Max. He was big but he was also very kind. "Okay, so I'm not an alien invader, Dooley. I'm just a mole and I'm here to tell you that I sympathize with you and your friends. If I was turned out of my own home by some intruder, I wouldn't be very happy about it either."

"Oh, we don't mind," said Max as he took a seat on the lawn. "We understand it's only a temporary arrangement. The moment Francine feels it's safe to leave we'll move back in."

"I wouldn't be too sure about that," said Jackie.

Now it was Max's turn to frown. At this point he'd been joined by two more cats: a white Persian and a hefty black specimen. All four of them were now eyeing her closely, and she was starting to feel distinctly crowded. So much so she was starting to wonder if she shouldn't have listened to Dave and kept her opinions to herself.

"What do you mean?" asked Max.

"Well, I know for a fact that I've seen this woman before. Though for the life of me I can't tell you where. All I know is that it was in connection with some unpleasantness. So I wanted to warn you not to let her bully you out of home and hearth but to fight back. Because before you know it, you'll be out on your ear, and she'll be settled in nice and comfy."

"She's just a friend in need of protection," the white Persian said. "What can be wrong with that?"

Jackie shrugged. "Just my personal opinion," she announced curtly. "Take it or leave it. It's no skin off my nose." She was starting to feel she had poked that very nose where it wasn't wanted.

"I think it's very noble of Odelia to give Francine a place to stay," said Brutus. "Okay, so I don't like that she doesn't like cats, but then we all know that some people are like that. You have cat lovers and cat haters, and apparently she's in the latter category."

"Or maybe she's allergic," the white Persian continued. "And that's not something she can do anything about. It's a medical condition, and not her fault at all, so we shouldn't hold it against her."

"Fine, fine," said Jackie, who was already seeing which way the wind was blowing. "If you feel it's all up to snuff, who am I to interfere, right? I just figured I'd give you guys the benefit of my experience. But if you don't want it, that's fine with me." So she held up her paw, and took her leave.

Cats, she thought. They were even worse than humans. Stubborn and superior, exactly like the humans they lived with. That's what you got when you lived in symbiosis with another species for a couple of millennia: you started resembling them in every way, their bad habits first and foremost.

As she dug down into the ground, eager to get away from four piercing pairs of cat eyes, she thought Max said something. But by then she was already burrowing down at a surprising rate of speed.

CHAPTER 8

"What was all that about, Max?" asked Dooley.

"She wanted to warn us," I said with a frown.

"Warn us about Francine," said Harriet.

"But why?" asked Brutus.

"She said she'd seen her somewhere before," I said, reiterating the mole's words. "And she said she was bad news, even though she couldn't remember where she had seen her."

"Oh, what does she know?" said Harriet. "She's probably mistaken. Moles are practically blind, did you know that? She must have taken a good look at Francine, didn't like what she saw, and developed one of those things against her. Um, starts with pre?"

"Prejudice?" I suggested.

"Exactly. A prejudice."

"Okay, so if she's a mole, then why did she tell me she was a genie?" asked Dooley, who was still processing this recent conversation with Jackie.

"She was simply pulling your leg," I said. "Genies don't

exist, Dooley, whether they come with a bottle attached to their person or an oil lamp or whatever."

"So she's not a genie, and she's not an alien invader?" Dooley asked, just to be on the safe side.

"She's a mole," I said. "Pure and simple." I didn't like that she had told us that Francine couldn't be trusted, though. Especially since Odelia had taken the woman into her home, pretty much kicked us out and told us to stay far away from her, and then gave her the best room in the house.

And then there was Chase, of course. He was in such a state that he couldn't protect his wife in case something happened. But then I dispelled the notion of danger from my mind. Like Harriet had said, moles possess pretty bad eyesight. It was very well possible that she hadn't recognized Francine at all, but had merely confused her with someone else entirely.

"She seemed nice, though," said Harriet now. "I've never met a mole before, but she seemed sincere when she told us she felt sorry for what happened to us."

"So why did you tell her it was all right?" asked Brutus.

Harriet shrugged. "You can't expect me to wash our dirty linen in public, can you? Whatever is going on with us is none of Jackie's business."

Dooley had studied Harriet closely. "What dirty linen do you want to wash, Harriet?" he asked now.

Harriet smiled. "Just an expression, Dooley. It means we don't discuss our private affairs with perfect strangers."

"She's not a perfect stranger, though, is she?" said Dooley. "She's our neighbor. Though technically she's Odelia's neighbor."

Just then, a face appeared in the opening in the hedge. It was Francine, and she seemed to be on the lookout for someone or something. When she saw us gathered nearby, she made a face and actually turned up her nose. But then she spotted Gran deadheading a rose bush and said, "It's Vesta, isn't it?"

Gran looked up, and when she saw that her granddaughter's guest desired speech, she plastered a pleasant smile onto her face. "That's right. How can I help you, honey?"

"The thing is that I'm afraid to use my phone, since I was being followed? But I urgently need to get in touch with my cousin. So could I perhaps use your phone?"

"Oh, absolutely," said Gran, getting up from the rubber mat she likes to use for gardening purposes. She took off her gardening gloves and took her phone out of the gardening apron she had tied on. "Here you go." She handed her phone to the woman, who took it with an effusive display of gratitude.

"I'll get it back to you as soon as possible," she assured Gran.

"Take your time," said Gran magnanimously, and went right back to her gardening duties.

Francine removed herself from the scene, and so naturally we decided to tag along to listen in on her conversation. Only we had to do it stealthily, since she disliked our presence to a great extent. And since I'm too big and noticeable, and Harriet is too pretty and sticks out wherever she goes, and Brutus is also too impressive as a presence, it was decided that Dooley should be the one to spy on our new house guest.

"Don't let her see you," Harriet admonished our friend.

"Don't let her hear you," Brutus added for good measure.

"And don't forget to remember everything you hear," I said.

Dooley seemed particularly ill at ease at having been sworn in as a feline spy all of a sudden, and he made this clear by giving us uncertain glances. "I don't know, you guys," he said finally.

"What don't you know, Dooley?" asked Harriet with an eye roll.

"I don't know if I can pull this off. Maybe you should go, Max. You're much cleverer than me."

"Yeah, but I'm also much bigger than you," I pointed out. "Not to mention very blorange. I'll stick out like a sore thumb."

He blinked a couple of times, then more or less graciously accepted his fate. "Oh, all right. But if she catches me, you have to come and save me, you hear?"

"She won't catch you," I said.

"Just make sure she doesn't see, hear or smell you," said Harriet. "And everything will be fine."

It was a tough proposition for one who's predisposed to be scared all the time that the sky will fall on top of his head. So to have to be some kind of feline James Bond definitely didn't sit well with him. But it was a testament to his determination to toe the line that he entered the battlefield, and, like a soldier going off to battle, took a deep breath, puffed out his chest, gave us the lingering wistful look of those who are about to die, and then ventured out.

"Brave soul," I said as we watched him go.

"Very brave," Brutus agreed with a respectful nod.

"Oh, it's just a simple little job," said Harriet. "How hard can it be?"

And so the long wait began. I just hoped our friend wouldn't muddle things up and forget to memorize the conversation as it transpired.

CHAPTER 9

Dooley didn't like this mission. In fact he didn't like it at all. But if Max asked him to do something, he would, even if he didn't think he was the right cat for the job. But it was definitely a mission that needed to be undertaken, and if no one else could do it, and he was the only one in a position to pull it off, go into the field as a feline spy he must. And so it was that he now snuck along the hedge that divided the backyards of both houses, hoping to remain concealed while putting himself into a position to listen in on Francine's conversation with her cousin Mike.

As luck would have it, Francine had decided to conduct her phone call right there, out in the open, rather than return to the house, where Dooley would have had a much harder time staying out of sight. The woman was pacing back and forth, with Dooley following her keenly from his hidden vantage point underneath the hedge. The call finally connected, and she said, "Mike! Oh, my God. Am I glad to hear your voice. I've been trying to reach you since this morning." She listened for a moment, then smiled. "No, I'm not on my phone. I thought it safer to borrow someone else's for now. Look, I've gone off the grid for a little while. At least until you manage to handle things on your end. I hope that's all right with you?"

It must have been all right with her cousin, for her smile widened, and she seemed to relax to some extent. "The reason I'm lying low is because after I left our meeting I was followed, can you believe it? Yeah, someone was following my car. I don't know how they found out, but somehow they did." She played with a ring on her finger for a moment, and smiled to herself as she listened to the other side of the conversation, which unfortunately Dooley couldn't hear. But it must have been something good, for she laughed. "That's very kind of you, Mike. I'm sure I'm safe. But you better hurry. And stay safe yourself."

After a few more exchanges, she finally disconnected, and thoughtfully tapped the phone against her chin. Which is when she noticed a molehill, and stomped on it. Then she saw another one, and stomped on that one as well. And before long, in an absentminded sort of way, she was moving from molehill to molehill and stomping them all back into their original position, leveling Jackie's hard work and collapsing the tunnels she had dug with such diligence. For some reason it made Dooley dislike Francine even more.

Even though he'd been mortally afraid of Jackie, he now saw that she was just another creature trying to make the most of things, and keeping herself and her family alive and in good health. And so what if she dug a few tunnels here and there, and redecorated the backyard to some extent? There was nothing wrong with that. Odelia and Chase's backyard wasn't exactly the Gardens of Versailles, after all.

Francine studied the phone Gran had given her, and now started checking something on the device, presumably surfing the web, Dooley thought. So far he didn't have a lot of shocking intel to relate to his friends, but he decided to hang in there for just a little while longer before he beat a retreat and reported back to Max and the others.

And he was just wondering idly where they were all going to sleep now that Francine had kicked them out of Odelia's place, when Gran's phone chimed and Francine immediately picked up. "Finally," she spoke into the phone. "It took you long enough. No, I've been holed up in this podunk town with the Kingsleys, just like we arranged. Yeah, the reporter for that local rag. Husband's a cop, but he's in a coma, so he won't be bothering us. So how soon can you get here?" She listened for a moment, then nodded to herself. "That's fine. I'll meet you there. And bring the merchandise. I want to take another look before I okay the transaction. And please don't let anybody see you, is that understood? It's bad enough that I have to lie low in this godforsaken place. We don't want to attract any unwanted attention from the locals."

Dooley frowned. Now what to make of this conversation? She hadn't named her correspondent, so Dooley had no idea who this person could possibly be. But it was probably safe to say it wasn't her cousin, since her entire demeanor had changed. As if she had suddenly turned into an entirely different person.

"Okay, so just do as you're told, Brian," she snapped into the phone. "Remember I'm still in charge. That's right. And get rid of the beard. You look like a clown in that thing."

She hung up with a vicious gesture, and crossed her arms for a moment, staring off into space with a deep frown on her face. She looks angry, Dooley thought. Not at all the kindly lady Odelia had taken into her home. But what was she up to? And who was this Brian person who had to get rid of his clown beard? And what was the stuff she wanted to inspect before the transaction?

It all sounded very mysterious to him. And so once he had determined she wasn't going to be conducting any more phone calls, he hurried back to where he came from, his three friends anxiously awaiting his return, and filled them in on the latest news.

"Okay, so she's meeting a guy with a clown beard," said Harriet, summing things up nicely. "Only when he gets here he won't have a beard. And also, he's going to bring something for her inspection."

"And he shouldn't forget that she's the boss," said Max thoughtfully.

"Oh, and she said she's staying in a podunk town. What's a podunk town, Max?" he asked.

Max grimaced. "It's not very complimentary, I can tell you that."

"She also didn't seem to think very highly of Odelia," said Dooley. "And she seemed glad that Chase is in a coma, so he can't bother her."

"A coma?" asked Brutus, his eyes widening considerably. "Did she actually use that word?"

"Yeah, she said Odelia's husband is a cop but he's in a coma, so he won't be bothering them."

"Oh, dear," said Max. "This isn't good, you guys."

"I'll say," said Brutus. "I didn't know Chase was in a coma."

"What's a coma?" asked Dooley.

"It's like sleeping, only more deeply," Harriet explained. "In fact it's such a deep sleep sometimes people don't ever wake up again."

Dooley stared at his friend. "Oh, no!"

"Oh, yes. But I don't think Chase is in a coma. Because if he was, Tex would have said something, and would have shipped him off to a hospital, where they can take better care of him than here at home."

"You did well, Dooley", said Max now, giving him a pat on the back. "In fact you did very well."

"Yeah, you did good," Brutus grunted approvingly.

Dooley immediately grew a few inches from all of this praise. "I don't think she saw me. She was too busy talking on the phone to notice me."

"Okay, so I never thought I'd say this," said Harriet, "but maybe the mole was right. Maybe this Francine is up to something."

"Yeah, but what?" asked Max. "And why did she pick our place of all places to lie low?"

"I don't know," said Harriet. "But we're going to find out, aren't we, you guys?"

Dooley's excitement waned. "Does this mean..." He gulped. "That I'll have to go and spy on her again?" He received three stolid nods in answer to his question, and made a face. "But I'm not a spy! I got lucky the first time, but she'll catch me next time for sure."

"I don't think so," said Max. "She's clearly too preoccupied to notice you, Dooley."

"Which means *you* should go and spy on her the next time," he suggested. "She won't notice you since she will be too busy inspecting this man's lack of clown beard." He gave his friend a hopeful look.

"You're probably correct," Max said, much to his relief. "And besides, she'll probably meet this person under the cover of darkness, which is why we should all make sure we're there when she does, so we can figure out what's going on with this woman."

"But how do we know when she'll meet this Brian character?" asked Harriet.

Max gave Dooley a smile. "Dooley will tell us."

"I will?" asked Dooley, much surprised.

"Yes, because you'll go back out there right now, and spy on Francine, and make sure you discover when exactly she will meet this person. And once you do, you will tell us, so we can prepare a plan."

Dooley's mood collapsed. More spying. More danger. Oh, no!

CHAPTER 10

Francine was in a funk. She could have been staying at a five-star hotel, or skiing in Switzerland, or lying on a beach in the Bahamas. But instead she had to lie low and be cooped up in this tiny house in the most boring town in the world with the most boring people. It was all she could do to be polite and spirit a smile onto her face every time Odelia was in the vicinity. Lucky for her the husband had suffered some kind of fatal collapse. It distracted Odelia's attention away from her guest and on the ailing hubby. For all intents and purposes a lucky break, after having suffered setback after setback for weeks.

She glanced in the direction of the house, and briefly thought she was being watched. But then quickly discarded the notion. Nobody was watching her here. Odelia had gone off to work, the husband was comatose, and the rest of the family were all doing whatever it was they did—living their boring lives in boringville, USA.

But very soon now she'd be out of there. Very, very soon, she hoped. Cause if she had to stay there even one more week, she'd go crazy and kill someone. And as she pictured

Mike Knight's stupid face and thought about the job she'd been contracted to carry out, she gave another molehill a vicious stomp.

* * *

MARGE HAD ARRIVED home from the library early for a change. She'd done some shopping and now was busy putting the groceries away in the fridge and the designated cabinets. When she closed the fridge, she found herself looking at four cats who seemed eager to have speech with her. She smiled at her sweethearts. "You guys are probably hungry, aren't you? How about a nice piece of chicken, mh?"

If she had expected them to yip with joy, she was sorely mistaken. Instead their expressions seemed to sour even more.

"We've got some bad news for you, Marge," said Max, acting as the group's spokesperson, as was his habit.

"Yeah, some very bad news," Harriet added.

Her face fell. "Oh, dear," she said as she took a seat on a kitchen chair. "Okay, so now that I'm sitting down, what is this news, and exactly how bad is it?"

"First off, Chase is in a coma," said Brutus. "Don't ask us how it happened, since we don't know, but apparently he is."

"Chase is in a coma?" she asked, bringing a distraught hand to her face. "But how—when?"

"Like I said, we don't know," said Brutus. "All we know is that he took a pill that Tex gave him, after he complained of feeling bad after eating a bad prawn, and so he fell asleep, and hasn't woken up since."

"Oh, no," said Marge, her mind a whirlpool of thoughts. Tex had told her something about Chase suffering from a mild case of indigestion, but this sounded like a great deal worse than simply an upset stomach. "What's the rest of the bad news?" she asked, afraid to hear it.

"Odelia has invited a woman to stay with them," said Max. "Her name is Francine Martin, and she's allergic to cats and spiders, so she had us kicked out, and she's been conducting mysterious phone calls."

"Francine Martin? And she's staying next door?" asked Marge. Odelia hadn't told her anything about a guest, which wasn't like her daughter. Usually Odelia always told her everything that was going on in her life. Since the two families lived next door from each other, and they were in and out of each other's houses all the time, it was hard to keep any secrets, even if Odelia wanted to, which she never did —until now.

"She says her life is in danger," said Harriet. "But now we're not so sure. All we know is that she's up to something —though we don't know what. Even Jackie told us, even though we didn't believe her."

"Jackie? Who's Jackie?"

"When I first met her I thought she was a genie," said Dooley. "And then I thought she was an alien invader, but now I know she's neither."

"Jackie is a mole who has moved in next door," Max explained. "She says she's seen Francine somewhere before, but doesn't remember where. But she also told us she's up to no good, even though she doesn't know what form this 'no good' might take."

"Oh, dear," Marge repeated as she took this all in. It certainly was a lot to process. And this processing part would have to wait, for at that moment her mother walked into the kitchen, and gave her an odd look.

"What's all this?" she asked. "Some kind of family meeting I wasn't informed about?"

"Something like that," Marge said. And in a few words she

told her mother about the story the cats had just told her. Ma was just as shocked as she was.

"Chase in a coma! But Tex said he's simply asleep."

"He might be asleep," said Max. "It's just that Francine seems to think he's in a coma. So maybe we should get a second opinion? From a doctor who isn't Tex?"

It was a difficult proposition, since bringing in a second doctor would upset Tex. But maybe Max was right. Maybe Tex had made the wrong diagnosis, and now Chase's life was in danger.

"Okay, do it," said Ma after a moment's thought, and Marge nodded. "But don't let him know."

"How am I supposed to do that?" asked Marge.

"Can't you distract him? Send him on some errand? Then by the time he comes back this doctor will have taken a good look at Chase, and depending on his diagnosis Tex will need to be told or not."

Marge thought for a moment. What errand could she send her husband on?

"You could always tell him to take us to the vet," Harriet suggested, eliciting groans from the other cats. "I mean, we all hate going to the vet, and Tex knows this as well as anyone. So if you tell him to take us, he'll know it's serious, and he won't suspect you're simply trying to get rid of him."

It was a species of excellent logic Marge hadn't expected from Harriet, and what's more, it just might work. "Okay, so maybe we'll follow your suggestion," she told Harriet. "I'll simply tell Tex that you ate something and now you're not feeling well, and can he please take you to see Vena as soon as possible."

"He'll want to know why you're not taking them," said Ma.

"I'll tell him I'm busy cooking dinner," said Marge.

"Okay. So why am I not taking them?"

"Because... you have to help me cook dinner."

"And what about Odelia?"

"She has to pick Grace up from daycare."

It seemed to settle things very nicely indeed. Now all they had to do was find a doctor who would be prepared to visit them at home at a moment's notice. But then she had just the right person in mind. Only trouble was that he was a good friend of Tex. But that couldn't be helped. She would just have to ask him to be discreet about his visit, and not tell his friend and colleague.

And so for the next few minutes she got on the phone with Cary Horsfield, who lived in Hampton Keys, and arranged for him to pay a house call. Then she got on the phone with Vena Aleman and made an appointment for the cats. And finally she called Tex and told him she needed him to take the cats to Vena.

The cats weren't too happy about it, especially Dooley, who lamented, "I keep having to sacrifice myself, you guys."

"It's all for the greater good, Dooley," said Max. "You want Chase to get better, don't you? Well, then."

Dooley clearly wasn't in the mood to think about the greater good. But that couldn't be helped. They had to think about Chase, and how they were going to get him healthy again. The rest didn't matter.

CHAPTER 11

Mike glanced out the window of his ancestral home and was pleased with the view. As far as the eye could see his gaze met with rolling fields and the odd copse of trees. To know that in this exact spot in his study his father had once stood, and his grandfather and great-grandfather, the Knight who had built the family home in the first place, struck him with a sense of awe and privilege. It also filled him with a certain anxiety, to know that the future of the Knight family now rested squarely on his shoulders. Sometimes it even felt like a burden that was entirely too heavy to bear. But fortunately he still had Dad, who might have retired several years ago, but was still available if he needed him and his sage advice and wisdom.

"You shouldn't have done it, son," his dad said now, seated in the armchair behind him. "It's not worth it, believe me."

"I had no other choice, Dad," he said, not for the first time, since they'd had this exact conversation several times before already.

"And I'm telling you that you do have a choice, and you

better make the right one, or you know what will happen to this family. It'll be the end of the line for us."

"Who do you think I'm doing this for?" he asked. "I'm trying to save this family, Dad. Save us from ruin."

"You should have said no," his dad insisted. "If only you'd talked to me first."

That ship had unfortunately sailed. Then again, if he had talked to his dad the old man would have asked him if he was out of his mind. He could have told him he was out of options, that's what he was. Out of options, out of time and out of funds.

"Look, it's not too late," said his dad, casting about for a solution. "We can still turn this around. We've been thrown a lifeline now so we should grab it and hold on to it and this will all go away."

"I wouldn't be too sure about that," he murmured. "You know as well as I do that it's not as easy as all that, Dad. These people don't mess around. They're in this for the long haul, and once they've dug in their claws they won't let go, whatever you say."

"Well, they have to! You have to make them!"

Mike Knight Senior swirled the last dregs of the amber liquid that was in his tumbler and downed it in one gulp. He looked old, Mike thought. Much older than his years. These recent developments hadn't done him any good. But then he had never fully recovered after Mom died. She had taken part of his health and a lot of his life's joy along with her. Mom had always been the backbone of the family, the hub around which everything revolved. When she passed, it hadn't merely made her husband a widower and her one and only son an emotional wreck, but it had thrown the entire family out of balance, and as a consequence Mike had made some bad choices. Though at the time he thought they were the right choices, of course.

"If we do what you suggest we'll have to sell the house," he now told his father. "We're going to need the money to invest."

"Never," said his dad determinedly, some of the old fire returning to his eyes. "I'll never sell this house, you hear me? My grandfather built this place with his bare hands, and I won't be the Knight that tears it down."

"But dad…"

"Over my dead body!"

That could probably be arranged, Mike thought. If push came to shove, and they followed his dad's advice, the financial hole they'd dig for themselves would be so big they might all perish in the aftermath.

"We'll find the money," said his dad. He pointed a finger at him. "*You'll* find the money. You have to."

Wasn't that the truth. It was his recklessness that had put his family in this precarious position and so it was only fair that he should be the one to drag them out of it again. But how?

"Pay the expert," said his dad. "Have him check the diary. And make sure no one finds out."

He nodded. It was the only way forward. The problem was that according to Francine people were already sniffing around. Following her after their meeting at the old mine. Once word spread about her find, things could only get worse. If Francine had to lie low, what would happen when the authenticity of that diary was confirmed? The pressure that would be brought to bear on him would be immense.

"Look, maybe this will pan out, and maybe it won't," he said. "But if it does, it won't be easy, Dad."

"I know, but you know I can handle myself, son," said his dad, putting on a brave face. "Can you?"

He grimaced. Now therein lay the rub. Was he prepared to play dirty? Cause the other side would. There was no doubt about that. But what other choice did he have? "You're right. It has to be done."

"Too darn right it does," said Dad with a grunt of satisfaction. "So what if we have to hire a couple of goons? It'll be worth it. And don't you worry about me. I've been through tougher challenges in my time."

He wasn't worried about his dad so much as he was about Emily. Once more he glanced out the window, and watched as his daughter spurred the horse she loved riding so much on to greater speeds. Even though she had only recently turned twelve, already his daughter was displaying a remarkable talent as a budding equestrian. If she kept this up she might qualify for her first competition as a child rider very soon. He had told his wife not to enter her in any competitions just yet, though. Even though he knew she possessed both the drive and the talent for show jumping, the sport she loved so much, he felt that at twelve she was too young. So he had decided to wait until she qualified as a junior rider, which would be the year she turned fourteen. By then she would have the maturity to enter any competition she liked.

Emily wasn't happy about his decision, but that couldn't be helped. He felt that she was simply too small, too fragile and too inexperienced for her age, no matter her passion for the sport of show jumping and her obvious talent. If anything happened to his daughter he would never forgive himself.

He turned away from the window. The die was cast. He'd consider Francine's proposal and do whatever it took to land a deal beneficial for his family. He'd do it so Emily could have a future.

CHAPTER 12

Sylvie watched Fury gallop at full speed, Emily spurring him on, and felt a pang of envy at the sight of the duo. Emily's cheeks were flushed with excitement, her eyes sparkled, and it was obvious to any observer that she was in her element. Horse and rider moved as one being as they flew across the terrain that Emily's dad had built at the Knight family estate. With the impressive family mansion as a backdrop, it wasn't too much to say that Emily had it all. She had the loving parents, the money and wealth that came with being one of Hampton Cove's most prominent families, and she had the talent and the beauty that would ensure she would lead a blessed life. The kind of life the likes of Sylvie could only dream of.

Her own life wasn't blessed at all. Not only had she been confined to a wheelchair since the accident, when she was six, but instead of a loving family all she had was her dad, since her mom had died in the same accident that had taken Sylvie's legs and dignity along with the hopes and dreams she had cherished from an early age. Whereas her best friend Emily always wanted to become an equestrian, Sylvie's dream had been to be a world-famous ballerina. And she might have achieved her dream, if a drunk driver hadn't crossed their SUV's path one night and crushed that dream and taken her mom away from them.

Emily's horse Fury performed the perfect vault across a natural barrier formed by a ditch and Sylvie clapped her hands in admiration. She might experience the odd pang of jealousy from time to time, but that had never stopped her from being her friend's most fervent cheerleader.

"Well done!" she shouted. "Well done, Em!"

Emily brought the horse around and dismounted, patting Fury affectionately across the flank. "You were amazing again, Fury," she said, panting a little from the exertion. "Simply amazing, boy."

"*You* were amazing," Sylvie said. "You were flying, Em!"

"I know," said Emily as she unclasped her helmet. As she removed it, she swept her long blond tresses across her shoulder, then tied them into a ponytail. "I think I'm almost ready, don't you?"

Sylvie grinned at her friend. "What are you talking about? You were born ready. You can do this, Em. You could enter any competition right now and you'd beat all of the other contestants."

"I'm not so sure," said Emily as she joined her friend. A stable boy had arrived to lead Fury back to the stables. The black stallion was going to be washed down and offered plenty of water to drink before being put back into his trusty stable where he could rest and recuperate from the exertion. After an hour or so he would also be fed. "My dad and I went to the Hampton Classic last week. Oh, to be riding Fury there one day, that would be so awesome, Sylv. You should have seen the winner. She was absolutely magnificent."

Sylvie wasn't sure whether her friend was referring to the rider or the horse. She assumed the former. "So why don't you enter one of the smaller competitions? See how it goes?" She had wheeled herself closer to where her friend had taken a seat on the paddock fence. "You have to start sometime, Em."

"Yeah, I know. But my dad says he'd like me to wait another two years until I can enter as a junior rider. He reckons I'm too small and delicate for my age, and it's too dangerous."

"Nonsense," said Sylvie fervently. "He's simply afraid you'll win, and then he won't be able to say no when you decide to turn this into a career, that's all."

"You may have a point," said Emily with a grin.

Emily and her dad had been involved in a long-protracted battle about her future. All she wanted was to enter the world of equestrianism and become a pro. Ride horses for a living, since it was all she was interested in, and she was good at it, too. But her dad had always felt it was just a passing phase. A hobby that had gotten out of hand and should be reined in. He wanted her to follow a normal career path: finish high school, enter college, before finally taking up a position in the family firm, only a very small part of which involved horses. As far as Sylvie could tell Mike Knight ran some type of consultancy company and the stables he housed on the family domain were a personal hobby of his. He did have a lot of horses, some of whom were used for breeding purposes. He even had a stable manager who took care of the animals.

The last thing Emily wanted was to follow in her father's footsteps, though, and fortunately for her she had her mother's support to go a different route and follow her dreams.

"You could always enter a competition under a false name," Sylvie suggested. "I'm sure your mom wouldn't mind setting that up."

Emily shook her head decidedly. "I could never get away

with it. The Knights are too well-known around here. I'd be discovered the moment I showed my face."

"You could enter a competition in a different part of the county. Like Westchester, maybe?"

Emily's face lit up at this. "Sylv, you're a genius!"

Sylvia shrugged. "I just happen to know that this Sunday there's a horse show in Pleasantville. There will also be a show jumping competition open to all ages. It's not part of the official US Equestrian curriculum but is set up by a local horse riding school. It would be the perfect opportunity for you to get some experience and for Fury to get used to being in an actual competition." She'd been studying the school's website last night and it looked perfect for Em and Fury. A chance to put both rider and horse through their paces in a fun and relaxed environment—no pressure.

"That's *exactly* what I need!" said Emily, hitting the palm of her hand with her fist. "I need to compete, Sylv, and get some actual experience. Otherwise what's the point? I can't expect to do this for a living if I don't even know if I can take the pressure of an actual competition, can I?"

"And I'll be right by your side the entire time," Sylv promised her friend. "And your mom, of course."

"Too bad Dad won't be there," said Emily. But then she shrugged. "His own fault for being such a stubborn so-and-so!"

"Well put!" said Sylvia.

And so it was decided. Emily would try to wheedle her mom into allowing her to go to Pleasantville and make sure her dad didn't find out, and so for the first time in her life her dream would finally come true: she would get to compete in an actual race!

"There's only one snag," said Sylvia. She didn't want to rain on her friend's parade, but there was one major problem with the plan she had to point out.

"What's that?"

"Well, the only way I can go is if my dad takes me, right? But that means I'd have to tell him, and you know my dad. He'll immediately start shooting his mouth off, and before you know it, your dad will find out, and that means it's bye-bye to that horse show for the both of us."

"Oh, no!" said Emily, bringing her hand to her mouth. "My dad *can't* find out, Sylv. No way. Isn't there anything you can do?"

"I could tell my dad I'm going off with you to some other place. And then he wouldn't have to know where I'm really going," she suggested. "Your mom wouldn't even have to know what we're up to," she added, knowing that Emily's mom would probably refuse to be a party to lying to Sylvia's dad, who was a close family friend.

"Then that's what we'll do," said Emily decidedly. "You'll tell your dad we're going shopping in Manhattan, and we'll tell Mom your dad is fine with the horse show thing, and Mom will tell Dad the same story you'll tell your dad, and we're all set!"

It sounded like the perfect ruse, and Sylvia was very excited that Emily had accepted the plan so eagerly. It would give her the opportunity to work out her own little plan. But then Emily didn't need to know about that, did she? She'd find out soon enough!

CHAPTER 13

A visit to Vena has never featured on our list of favorite pastimes. Quite the opposite, in fact. If ever there was a hell for cats, it would probably look like Vena Aleman's office. This veterinarian has given me so many nightmares that I've stopped counting them. Only this time there wasn't actually anything wrong with us, so that probably meant we wouldn't be subjected to her usual jabs and probes. Though of course with Vena you never knew. Veterinarians have this uncanny knack for identifying any situation as the perfect opportunity to start practicing their needlework skills.

And so it was with clenched butt cheeks that the four of us rode in Tex's car on our way to the vet.

"What is Tex going to tell Vena?" asked Harriet. "I mean, he has to tell her something, right?"

"Marge told him to tell Vena that we've all been feeling a little under the weather lately," I said. "It's vague enough so Tex wouldn't suspect anything, but at the same time it will give Vena something to do."

"I have been suffering from a mild toothache," said

Brutus, bringing a paw to his jaw. "Nothing serious, mind you," he was quick to add. "But I might tell Vena to take a look, just to be sure."

"And how are you going to do that?" asked Harriet. "Vena doesn't speak our language, remember?"

"I could always point to my tooth," Brutus suggested. "You know, give her a sad look and point?"

"Yeah, that'll do the trick," said Harriet, but I could tell she was kidding. Vena might be an ace vet, but like most humans she's terrible at picking up those subtle hints we give her.

Tex studied me through the rearview mirror. "Odelia was right," he said. "You look a little sick, Max. I hope you won't come down with something serious. Good thing you have the support of your friends. And I'll be holding your paw throughout the procedure, of course." He gave me a look that was probably supposed to reassure me, but instead it only served to frighten me out of my wits!

"Me!" I cried. "Why me?!"

"I thought Marge said Vena was going to examine all of us?" asked Harriet, confused.

"Marge and Odelia must have gotten their wires crossed," said Brutus. He gave me a toothy grin. "But know that we're all there for you, buddy. And Tex will be holding your paw."

"I don't need anyone to hold my paw!" I cried. "I need this car to turn back!"

"It's probably true that of the four of us you're the one in the worst condition, Max," said Harriet. "So it stands to reason that Vena will want to take a closer look at you. I mean, look at me. I'm the picture of health. Tough to fool Vena into believing there's anything wrong with me."

"Same here," Brutus grunted. "I've never felt better in my life."

"But I feel great!" I said. "I don't need to be examined!"

"Famous last words," Brutus said with an evil grin. He

clearly was relieved that he wasn't the one being put on the spot!

"It's all of that lard that's attached itself to your waistline, Max," said Harriet helpfully. "We all know that body fat is the worst kind of fat. Bad for your heart. So it's probably a good thing Vena will take a good look at you."

"I'm healthy," I insisted. The truth was that I was starting to see that Vena, being the devious minx that she is, would probably find something wrong with me, and would suggest I come back for a second visit, and then a third, and a fourth, and so on and so forth. And before long I'd resemble a pincushion!

"You just told us you're suffering from a toothache, Brutus," I said. "So you should be the one Vena examines." I was getting desperate here, and was starting to contemplate avenues of escape from the car.

"Actually the pain in my tooth is gone," said Brutus. "Odd how that works, isn't it?"

Dooley had placed a paw to my brow, and was regarding me with a look of concern. "Are you running a fever, Max?" he asked. "Cause you look a little hot under your collar."

"I don't look hot under my collar," I said with some heat. "I'm blorange, so hot is my natural color!"

"Still," Harriet insisted. "I think this visit will do you a world of good."

"Yeah, just take one for the team, Maxie," said Brutus. "Do it for Chase."

I freely ground my teeth together. This wasn't my idea of 'taking one for the team.' And Chase's situation wouldn't be improved in any way by sacrificing myself 'for the team,' as Brutus called it. Then again, since everyone seemed to be in agreement, I guess I was simply going to have to grin and bear it.

It didn't take us long to arrive at Vena's palace of horrors, and we were let into the waiting room, where a woman with two gerbils, another woman with a Golden Retriever and a man with a goldfish in a bowl sat looking sad and resigned to their fate. The pets, I mean. Not the humans.

It looked like we were in for a long wait...

After about five hours of biding our time—though it could have been forty-five minutes—we were ushered into Vena's inner lair, where she keeps her instruments of torture sharp and ready for duty.

She gave me a commiserating sort of look as Tex explained to her what was allegedly ailing me, then invited Odelia's dad to hoist me up onto the metal examination table, and commenced with the prods I remembered so well from the last time I was there.

Prods in the stomach. Prods in the ribs. Her fingers were everywhere all at once, and I would have laughed since I'm ticklish and if the process had been remotely enjoyable, which I must insist it wasn't!

"Mh," she said finally, as she prized open my mouth with her fingers and took a good long look at my tonsils and possibly all the way down to the contents of my bowels. Vena is a formidable woman, built along the lines of a Sherman tank, and so I knew that resistance was futile. I still lodged a verbal protest by mewling in what I hoped was a piteous fashion. I knew it wouldn't work on Vena herself, since she's devoid of the finer feelings most humans share like compassion and empathy. But it might work on Tex, who might be induced to stay Vena's hand if he was so moved.

"So how is he?" asked Tex with a touch of solicitousness.

"I don't like these spots," said Vena. She was showing something to Tex, who gasped in shock. It made me a little weak in the knees, I must admit. Nobody likes their human to gasp like Tex did!

"Ringworm," said Tex immediately.

"My conclusion exactly, colleague," said Vena grimly.

"My wife did tell me he's been scratching himself a lot lately."

"Do your cats spend a lot of time outdoors?" asked Vena. She had turned on a powerful lamp and was now studying me more closely, like one would a microbe under a microscope.

"Yes, they do. We have a backyard, and they're free to move around."

"Mh," the vet said emphatically, and the way she said it made it clear she didn't approve of this liberty at all. For a moment I was afraid she was going to suggest locking me up inside and never letting me out again. But lucky for me she didn't jump to this extreme conclusion. Instead she said, "Yup, it's ringworm, all right." She now turned her beady eye on my three friends, who were on the floor waiting with bated breath. "Let's get the others up here," she suggested.

And so my friends were also subjected to the same close scrutiny I had been subjected to. The upshot was that all four of us suffered from the same malady, namely the dreaded ringworm that had attached itself to our noble physiques.

The treatment was simple: a topical anti-fungal medicine to be applied to the infected areas and a second medicine to be imbibed as well. The treatment would possibly take six weeks or more, and would have to be repeated to get rid of the nasty little beasts. The fact that we all lived together seemed to have been a factor in the spread of the disease. Apparently we had all infected one another. Gasp!

"Oh, this is bad," said Harriet once we had been released from captivity and Tex was seated at Vena's desk to listen to the verdict and pay the fine. "This is so bad. I look like a monster, you guys!"

"You don't look like a monster," said Brutus. "But it's true that it's not a nice thing to be suffering from. At least now I know why I was so itchy all the time."

"Same here," I said moodily. A little itch has never hurt anyone, but it was certainly true that lately I'd been more itchy than usual.

"I wonder who could have given me this monstrous parasite," said Harriet. Clearly she had left the self-pitying stage and entered the blaming stage. "Must be either Shanille or Clarice. Probably Clarice. She spends all of her time rooting through dumpsters. I saw her last week, you know. She was prancing up and down Main Street, and we chatted for a while. One of these things must have jumped from her to me."

"It's a fungus," said Brutus. "Not a flea or a louse."

"Then it's a lousy fungus," said Harriet. "And I hate it."

"What if we don't take this medicine?" asked Dooley.

"Then all of your hair will fall out," I said.

Harriet gasped in horror. "Oh, no!"

"That's what Vena just said," I reminded her.

"I wasn't listening," she said sadly. "I was too shocked when she said I was suffering from the same thing you're suffering from, Max." She narrowed her eyes. "When I see Clarice, I'll give her a piece of my mind. Just you wait and see!"

"If it was Clarice, she should probably come and see Vena as well," I said. "Otherwise she'll infect other cats, not to mention her hair might fall out, too."

"Well, I don't mind," said Harriet. "Serves her right for infecting us!"

"It's not Clarice's fault, Harriet," I said. "Any cat can get ringworm. It's something very common. Or at least according to Vena it is."

"Will my hair fall out, Max?" asked Dooley. "Only I don't

think I'll look very nice without my hair. I think I'll look very silly. Plus I will be very cold at night."

"None of us will lose their hair," I assured him. "With this treatment we'll get rid of this fungus and we'll be just fine."

"Though it could have been Shanille, of course," said Harriet, still desperately trying to find out where to put the blame for her predicament. "I was standing awfully close to her last night."

"This didn't happen overnight," I assured her. "It takes time for the fungus to develop and spread to this extent. It's possible we've been carrying this for weeks already."

"At least Vena found it," said Brutus. "As much as I hate to admit it, it's a good thing we came, and even better if she can get rid of this stuff."

He was right. Even though none of us particularly liked Vena, it was true that she had her uses. And even though this visit hadn't been planned, it was good that Harriet had suggested it to Marge as a ruse. So it was actually Chase's condition we had to thank for this. And I fervently hoped this doctor Horsfield Marge had called in to take a look at the sick cop would be as efficient and thorough as Vena and would find the cause of the mysterious malady that was plaguing him.

"Do you think Chase is suffering from the same ringworm, Max?" asked Dooley.

"I very much doubt it," I said. "Ringworm doesn't put you in a coma. Something else does."

"Let's hope he's fine," said Brutus.

And so we all crossed our digits and hoped for the best.

CHAPTER 14

To say that Marge was worried about Chase would be an understatement. Especially if it transpired that her own husband was somehow to blame for the young man's predicament. She had told Odelia about her plan to ask for a second opinion, and her daughter had hurried home so she would be there when Cary Horsfield arrived. Tex was at Vena's with the cats, and Francine was out in the backyard talking on the phone, as she seemed to do a lot.

When the doorbell rang it was Marge who opened it, since she was the one who had asked for this urgent home visit from the medical man. The fact that he was one of Tex's colleagues had given rise to a certain measure of embarrassment. But she had explained it away by telling Doctor Horsfield that Tex was away and Chase was in a bad way.

"Hello, Marge," said the doc when she opened the door. Cary Horsfield was a man of about her own age, with thinning gray hair and a long narrow face not unlike a horse. The only difference was that he was wearing glasses, which Marge had never seen a horse do.

"Hello, Cary," she said in tremulous tones. Even after

having been married to a doctor for twenty-five years, she still experienced the intense relief when being in the presence of a man who might be able to make all of her troubles go away. "He's upstairs."

"Let's take a look, shall we?" said Cary, displaying all the hallmarks of a good doctor by having the look (reassuringly bland) and the voice (reassuringly sonorous) and the presence (reassuringly soothing) required for the position. And she knew from experience and Tex's endorsement over the years that Cary Horsfield was among the best the profession had to offer, so Chase was definitely in good hands.

Odelia and Marge's mom were already present in the room where the ailing cop lay, and Cary gave them both a curt nod in greeting. His eyes were immediately drawn to the patient, and as he placed his doctor's bag on a chair, he took a seat on the bed and began his examination of Marge's son-in-law. After having listened to his heart, checked his blood pressure, and examined his pupils by shining a little light in them, the frown he displayed made Marge's heart perform a light canter in her chest. She recognized that frown from having seen it on her own husband's face many times. It was a frown that didn't bode well.

"Well," said Cary finally. "He's in a coma, all right. You were right about that. So why hasn't he been transferred to a hospital, Marge?"

"We weren't sure what he was suffering from," Marge said.

"We thought he was asleep," Odelia supplied.

"He ate a bad prawn last night," Ma said. "So Tex gave him a sleeping pill."

Cary's frown deepened. "I don't see the logic, I'm afraid. If Chase was suffering from indigestion, why give him a sleeping pill?"

Marge shrugged. "It seemed like a good idea at the time,"

she said in tremulous tones. Oh, dear. Not only had her husband failed to make the correct diagnosis, but that sleeping pill may have induced Chase's coma and put Odelia's beloved husband in this terrible state.

"I better call an ambulance," said Cary. "He needs to be monitored around the clock."

"Is he… in a very bad way, doctor?" asked Odelia. There was a catch in her voice, and Marge could tell she was extremely worried, as they all were.

"His vital signs appear to be fine," said Cary with a reassuring smile. "But I still feel he should be admitted for specialized treatment. We don't know what exactly put him in this coma, and coma patients are tricky. You never know how they're going to respond. So it's imperative that he receive the best care."

"Of course," said Marge.

"So his vital signs are fine?" asked Odelia hopefully.

"Yes, as far as I can tell he seems to be all right," said Cary. "But like I said, coma patients need to be monitored closely. To leave him like this would constitute gross negligence on my part." He directed a stern look at Marge, and she knew exactly what that look meant. The gross negligence was on the part of her husband.

Oh, dear, she thought. If Tex lost his license, what were they going to do? It was too horrible to contemplate. But then she immediately told herself that Chase's health was what they should be concerned about right now, not any possible consequences for Tex further down the line.

The ambulance was called, and before long a stretcher was brought up the stairs, and Chase carried down by two particularly burly paramedics—which was necessary since Chase was a big man.

"It breaks my heart to see him like this," Odelia confided

to her mother. "He got so much worse in such a short time. It's scary."

"It is scary," Marge confirmed. "And all because of a bad prawn? I don't understand."

"Why didn't Dad..." But she didn't finish the sentence. It was something they were all wondering right now. Why hadn't Tex seen the signs? Why hadn't he seen that Chase was in such a bad way that he needed to be transferred to a hospital ASAP?

"I just don't understand," said Ma as she shook her gray head. "With a doctor in the house you'd think you're safe, and now this."

The paramedics had transferred the stretcher into the waiting ambulance, and Odelia decided to ride with them to the hospital. Marge and her mother promised to join her as soon as possible. But they also had Grace to think about. And Marge didn't want to leave Francine alone in the house either. That didn't seem right, especially since they didn't really know the woman. So arrangements would have to be made.

She watched the ambulance drive off with flashing light and wailing siren, and as she turned back, she saw that up and down the street pretty much the whole neighborhood had emerged from their homes to see what was going on. Her next-door neighbors Marcie and Ted were the first ones to address her.

"What's going on with Chase?" asked Marcie. "Is he going to be all right?"

"I don't know," said Marge honestly. "He's in a coma, and we don't know when he will wake up."

"It's a terrible business," Ma said. "I'll go and look after Grace, shall I, honey?"

"Thanks, Ma," said Marge.

"Such a strong and healthy young man," said Marcie. "I

just can't believe he would suddenly fall into a coma like that. How did it happen?"

"We think he ate a bad prawn last night. So he was up half the night feeling sick and unable to go to sleep. This morning he said he was feeling better, so he went to the gym, but he suffered a relapse, so he came home and went to bed instead of going to work. Next thing we knew he wouldn't wake up."

She decided not to mention the part about the sleeping pill Tex had given their son-in-law. She didn't want to feed the rumor mill that kind of potentially damaging information.

"A bad prawn," said Marcie. "How about that?"

"I ate a bad prawn once," said Ted. "I was up sick the whole night. Remember, honey? I haven't eaten prawns since. The smell alone is enough to make my stomach turn."

"You eat prawns," said Marcie. "You ate them last week."

"I did not," said Ted. "Unless I didn't know it was a prawn," he added, hedging his bets. "They probably put prawns in everything these days, just like sugar. And before you know it, you're sick as a dog and you don't even know why."

"There's nothing wrong with prawns in general," said Marcie. "It's the bad ones you need to look out for. It just takes one."

"Exactly," said Ted. "It's the bad ones that will kill you."

The conversation wasn't exactly conducive to her peace of mind, so Marge excused herself and returned indoors. She wanted to be where her daughter was, to make sure Chase was all right. But she also needed to be home when her husband got back from the vet with the cats, so she could break the news to him about what his colleague had said. He wouldn't be happy that they had called in a second doctor, but that couldn't be helped. At least Chase would get all the help he needed, and that was what mattered most.

As she entered the house, and walked through to the kitchen, she saw that Francine was pacing Odelia's backyard, still talking on the phone. She wondered briefly what could be so important that she would spend an hour on the phone. But then figured she had more important things to deal with, and started rooting through the fridge in search of the remnants of last night's dinner. Good thing she never threw anything away. Possibly—or even probably—the hospital would want to analyze the prawns that had put Chase in such a state.

She put the leftovers in a ziplock plastic baggie and put it in the fridge. The moment Tex got back, she would take it to the hospital so they could have it examined at the lab and the culprit identified.

The odd part was that they had all eaten those prawns: she, Tex, Odelia, Ma... Even her brother Alec and his girlfriend Charlene had been over last night, and had also eaten those same prawns.

And none of them had suffered any consequences.

Like Marcie had said: it only took one bad prawn.

CHAPTER 15

"Ringworm?" asked Vesta as she studied her four cats. "What's ringworm?"

"It's a kind of fungus," her son-in-law explained. "Symptoms are circular areas of hair loss and scaly, red patches of inflamed skin. But not to worry," he added with a reassuring smile. "It's perfectly treatable, and in fact Vena has already started the treatment. Now all we have to do is continue and the spots will disappear like snow before the sun."

They were in the kitchen, where Vesta had brought Grace. She now wondered if they shouldn't separate the cats from the little girl, just in case this ringworm was infectious. Grace had a habit of playing with the cats, and that didn't seem like a good idea right now.

She watched as Grace now crawled over to the cats, and immediately picked the toddler up. "Let's get you somewhere safe," she said as she led the little girl away. She gave her daughter a knowing look, and Marge nodded. She had understood the message. She didn't want to say in front of the cats that they couldn't be in the same room as Grace for the time being—they might get upset.

So she took Grace into the living room, but not before firmly closing the kitchen door so the four cats couldn't follow them. This was going to be a little difficult, since they had never had to restrict the cats' movements before. They simply weren't used to it, and always considered the house their own—which of course it was.

So how were they going to handle this? Francine hated cats, and didn't want them in the house with her. But now that they had ringworm, they couldn't be anywhere near Grace either. And since Grace's mom and dad were at the hospital, someone needed to look after the little girl.

"It's going to take some organizing," she told Grace, who had settled down on the carpet and was playing with her favorite doll. "But I'm sure we'll work something out. And as soon as the cats are fine again, you can play with them as much as you want."

Grace stared at her with those big seaweed-colored eyes of hers—the same eyes as her mother—and Gran smiled. She was such a lovely little girl, and it pained her to know that her daddy was laid up in a hospital bed right now, and might never wake up again.

But then she told herself she shouldn't think like that. Of course Chase would wake up again. He was a strong young man, and in perfect health. No silly little prawn was going to get the better of him. At least for Grace's sake she fervently hoped it wouldn't.

* * *

MARGE HAD ASKED her husband to take a seat at the kitchen table. It was time to lay it all out for him. "Chase is in the hospital," she said, not seeing any point in beating about the bush.

"The hospital!" Tex cried, shooting up from his chair.

"I was so worried about him I called Cary Horsfield, Tex. He came over and he said Chase should be transferred to the hospital immediately. And he also said he didn't understand why the decision hadn't been taken sooner, since the hospital is the only place where they can monitor him and make sure he's okay."

Tex stared at her. "You called Cary Horsfield?"

"Yes, I did," she said with a touch of defiance. "I was worried about Chase, and I felt—we all felt—that we needed a second opinion."

Tex took it better than Marge had expected. Instead of becoming upset, he nodded. "You did the right thing."

"I did?"

"Of course. If I were you I would have done exactly the same. Called in another doctor to ask for a second opinion." He had sunk down on the chair again and rubbed his eyes. "I don't know what happened, Marge. I should have seen how seriously ill Chase was. I should have been the one to send him to the hospital."

She placed a hand on his shoulder. "You were afraid they might conclude that you put him in that coma," she said softly. "By giving him that sleeping pill."

Tex nodded. "I should never have given him that pill. But I checked it before I took the cats to the vet, and it was exactly that: a sleeping pill. And a mild dose, too. Nothing that could ever put anyone in a coma. So I don't understand, Marge. I really don't. I mean, the man suffered from indigestion, for God's sakes. And when he couldn't sleep, I decided to give him a light sedative."

"He must have had a bad reaction to the sedative."

"Impossible," said Tex. "It's a harmless drug."

"I'm sure they'll subject him to a thorough examination at the hospital. They'll figure out what happened and how to deal with it." At least she hoped they would. What if Chase never woke up from his coma again? You heard about cases like that all the time. It was too awful to bear thinking about.

"Do you think... he'll wake up again?" she asked.

But Tex was staring before him, lost in thought.

"Is Chase going to be all right?" asked Dooley.

The four cats had been unusually quiet ever since they got back from the vet. They had sat on the floor, drinking everything in, and hadn't said a single word, which was not like them. They usually were a very talkative bunch—especially Harriet. But even the white Persian seemed impressed by these recent events.

"I don't know, Dooley," she said truthfully.

"How can he be in a coma?" asked Brutus. "He's such a big, healthy guy. And he's always in the gym, pulling weights. Or pushing them. Or whatever he does with them."

"I think he alternates between pushing and pulling," said Max. "It depends on what muscle he's training."

It all seemed irrelevant right now. Chase might never be in that gym again for all they knew.

"There's something else I need to tell you," said Marge, figuring she might as well break all the bad news in one go. "Since you guys have ringworm it's better if you don't go near Grace for a little while. At least until you're all feeling better and the infection can't spread."

The four cats looked at her with astonishment written all over their features. "We can't go near Grace again?" asked Harriet finally. "But why?"

"Ringworm is an infectious disease," she explained. "So you could pass it on to Grace if you're not careful." They could pass it on to the rest of the family as well, of course, so measures would have to be taken. "For now I think you should all be confined to the same space if possible. So let's say you won't go upstairs and restrict your movements to the ground floor. I'm going to have to wash all the beddings, clothes, things you guys were in contact with. And I'll sanitize all the surfaces you touched with bleach." She smiled. "Just think of it as a big spring cleaning." Even though it wasn't spring.

"It's the worms, isn't it?" said Dooley. "You're afraid we'll pass our worms on to you."

"Ringworm isn't actually a worm," said Marge. "It's a fungus. But it's still infectious, and should be treated to stop the spread." When she saw the sad faces on her cats, she added, "Oh, cheer up, you guys. It's not the end of the world. Before you know it, you'll be right as rain again."

"Is it… deadly?" asked Brutus.

"No, it is not. Though if left untreated it does cause quite a nasty rash. So let's count ourselves lucky that we caught it in time."

"So to sum things up," said Max. "Chase is in a coma right now, and might never wake up again. The four of us have been infected with a nasty fungus and aren't supposed to come anywhere near you guys, or spend time in our favorite places—and that includes next door, since Francine hates us. And Tex might lose his license to practice medicine because he failed to correctly diagnose what's going on with Chase."

Marge had slumped a little. "Yeah, that sounds about right."

"You forgot one thing, Max," said Dooley softly.

"I did?"

Dooley nodded. "Alien invaders are crawling all over our backyard, digging tunnels and preparing to take over the planet."

CHAPTER 16

The time had come to organize a meeting, and so we all headed out through the pet flap and reconvened behind the garden shed, which was one of Tex's favorite haunts but now stood empty, since the good doctor was in a heap of trouble and so was the rest of the family. Once upon a time the paterfamilias had used the garden house to engage in one of his hobbies, namely the painting of fruits and vegetables, also known as freggies. But that episode, along with many others, unfortunately hadn't had a happy ending. I just hoped that this particular episode, which was a lot graver in every way, would.

"We have to discuss this," said Brutus. "And we have to put it to a vote."

"What vote?" I asked.

"Whether we still want to be part of this family or not," said Brutus, and judging from the expression on his face he wasn't kidding.

"What do you mean?" asked Dooley. "Of course we are a part of this family. That's what families are, right? And we're it. Or they are it. And we are part of it."

"Dooley, nobody can force you to be part of a family if you don't want to be," Brutus explained. "And it's becoming more and more clear to me that this family doesn't want us, so why would we want them?"

"They do want us," I said. "They just don't want us around. There's a difference."

"Semantics, Max," Brutus argued. "They don't want us around because they don't really want us. So I say we move out and find ourselves a different family."

"Oh, Brutus, please stop talking," said Harriet. "Cause what you're saying doesn't make any sense."

"Of course it does!" said our butch friend. "It makes perfect sense. Didn't you hear Marge just now? We can't go upstairs, we can't come anywhere near them, she will have to clean the entire house with bleach... If that's not a hint that we should take a hike I don't know what is."

"It's the fungus she doesn't want," I pointed out. "Not us."

"It's the same thing," Brutus argued. "The fungus is part of us now, and if they can't learn to love the fungus, we should take a hint and move out."

I could tell that Brutus was deeply insulted by Marge's new rules, but I could have told him that it wasn't about us, but about protecting the ones that hadn't been affected by the ringworm yet. And also, she was doing this for us as well, since what was the point of getting rid of the infection if we could simply get re-infected again? But Brutus wasn't having it.

"Chase's mom lives in New York. I say we go and live with her. I know for a fact that she always adored me, and so did Chase's aunt."

"So why did she give you to Chase?" I asked.

Brutus shrugged. "Lack of space, mainly. They live in a small flat, and also, Chase's mom is suffering from Alzheimer's, so taking care of her takes a lot of his aunt."

"If she couldn't cope with you, what makes you think she'll want to cope with the four of us?"

This gave him some food for thought. "Okay, so maybe someone else will take us? There must be thousands of people who love cats and who'll provide a new home for us."

"Oh, Brutus," said Harriet with an eye roll. "Be reasonable."

"I am being reasonable! It's our future we need to think about here."

"This is not the time to throw a hissy fit," said Harriet. "Chase is in the hospital, and there's a stranger living next door, and Tex might be in trouble over what happened to Chase. So instead of making things even more difficult for the Pooles we should all rally around. Give them a helping paw!"

It was sound advice, and even though I had no idea what we could possibly do about either of the set of circumstances that had conspired to put our family in such a state of turmoil, I knew they needed all the support they could get. Even Brutus seemed to realize that perhaps he'd spoken too soon.

"Okay, so maybe we'll keep our situation under advisement," he said finally. "Wait and see how things play out. But I'm still deferring judgment, you understand? And if I don't like what I see, I'm out of here."

"You be out of here," said Harriet. "But I'm staying put. Our family needs us now more than ever, Brutus. So let's figure out what's going on, all right?" She turned to me. "Max, what are your thoughts?"

Frankly I didn't have any thoughts, except for the fact that it was obvious things weren't going so well. "Like you said, we have to be there for our family. Which is a little hard since we're not allowed anywhere near them until this medication kicks in and kicks the ringworm out."

"There has to be something we can do," said Harriet. "What do you think, Dooley?"

Dooley stared at her. "You're asking me what I think?"

"Yes, what are your ideas about what's going on?"

Dooley's lips opened and closed a couple of times, and finally he said, "I think Chase was poisoned. And I think it's the aliens that did it."

We all groaned. "Okay, thanks for your input, Dooley," said Harriet. "Anyone else want to share their ideas? Now is the time, people."

But unfortunately no brainwave would come, and that seemed to apply to the rest of the small gathering as well.

And so the meeting was adjourned and we still weren't anywhere closer to a solution to the many problems that vexed us.

Harriet and Brutus went off to go for a walk so they could gather their thoughts, and Dooley and I decided to do the same thing.

"I didn't want to say this in front of the others, Max," said Dooley. "But I think I have an idea how we should proceed."

"Oh?" I said. "And what is that idea?"

"We need to take a closer look at the aliens," he said. "Things started going wrong the moment they set foot in our backyard, Max. And that can't be a coincidence."

I mused on this for a moment, but finally I had to agree. "I think you're absolutely right, Dooley."

"I am?" he asked, much surprised.

"So let's go and have a chat with Jackie, shall we? See what she has to say for herself."

Dooley gulped. "Are you sure, Max? Is it… safe?"

I gave him a reassuring smile. "I'm sure it is. And when you feel threatened, you can always threaten to unleash that ringworm on her. That should make her think twice, wouldn't you agree?"

The thought of unleashing the ringworm on the aliens seemed to please him to no end, and so it was decided: we would interview Jackie, and find out what she knew about these strange events.

CHAPTER 17

People who suffer from moles in their backyard may have told you this: even though they seem to be everywhere, at the same time they're also nowhere to be found. In fact when you actually want to clap eyes on the mole that has been turning your pristine lawn into a plowed field fit for planting potatoes, you'll discover they're very elusive creatures. We'd been crawling all over that backyard for twenty minutes, calling out Jackie's name and inspecting the impressive number of molehills that she had erected, when finally one of these hills stirred, and a tiny head suddenly appeared.

"What do you want?" she asked, sounding a lot less forthcoming than the last time we met.

"We just want to talk," I assured her.

"But if you touch me, I'll give you ringworm!" Dooley warned.

Jackie's glittering eyes fastened on Dooley, then she said, "I'll take your ringworm and I will raise you Lyme disease, rocky mountain spotted fever, anaplasmosis and tularemia."

Dooley gulped. "What?!" he cried.

"These are some of the diseases moles habitually carry," Jackie explained. "So don't mess with me, Smith Jones, or I will mess you up."

"My name is actually Dooley," Dooley confessed.

Jackie smiled. "I know. I was just messing with you."

"I want to ask you a very important question," said Dooley. "Are you invading our planet, Jackie?"

Jackie made a funny guttural sound. It took me a moment to recognize it as giggling. "The only place I'm invading right now is this backyard. The rest of the planet will have to wait."

"Oh, okay," said Dooley.

"You know, I think I like Smith Jones better. Dooley is such a silly name. Then again, you are a silly cat, so maybe it's fitting."

Dooley scowled at the mole, but if the thought had entered his mind to transfer his ringworm to her, I don't think he stood a chance. Moles are fast. One move and she would have popped back down and disappeared into the maze of tunnels she had dug.

"Okay, what we wanted to talk to you about," I said, "I don't know if you've noticed, but Chase has been taken to the hospital. Apparently he's in a coma, so things are really serious. And if he doesn't make it, and even if he does, chances are that Tex will lose his license, which means he'll be out of a job, and become something of a local pariah. Some of his patients might even sue him for damages, and there will be no end of trouble ahead if that happens. Not to mention the fact that we will probably have to move. Maybe to an entirely different part of the country."

I noticed that Dooley was staring at me. "Move to a different part of the country? Max!"

"If Tex is accused of administering the drug that put Chase in this coma, losing his license to practice medicine will be the least of his problems. People have a habit of pointing the finger, Dooley, and every patient Tex has ever had is going to start wondering if he made some mistake somewhere down the line that caused them some problem. And they'll come after him. That's just the way these things go."

"But I don't want to move, Max!"

"Nobody wants to move, Dooley. Which is why we need to get to the bottom of this thing. Cause I just can't believe that Tex would do such a thing, even inadvertently. He may be a little goofy, but he's good at what he does. And he loves Chase like a son."

"Chase is his son."

"Son-in-law."

Jackie had been following the back-and-forth with interest, and now said, "Remember when I told you I thought I'd seen this Francine person somewhere before?"

"Yes, I do," I said.

She seemed surprised. "I thought you weren't listening."

I smiled. "I'm a cat, so I'm always listening, Jackie, even when it looks like I'm not."

"Okay, so I've been giving this a lot of thought, cause I just hate it when I can't remember something. It just keeps nagging at me. And I think I finally figured it out."

"You have?"

She nodded. "This isn't my first rodeo, you know. I've been in other backyards of other homes, and what they all have in common is that the homeowner usually isn't all that welcoming when we arrive to do our business. Some are more hostile than others, and once upon a time I even encountered a homeowner who thought of nothing better to do than to stick firecrackers in the tunnels we'd dug and light them up. It made a terrible racket, and he blew up half of his own backyard. We didn't stick around after that, as you can imagine."

"No, I can imagine that wouldn't be a nice experience," I said, hoping she would get to the point soon.

"Okay, so that particular homeowner reminds me a lot of your Francine."

"But… didn't you just say he was a male?"

"I did, but he reminded me of her a lot. So maybe the two of them are related?"

"Okay." I thought about this for a moment. It was possible, of course. Or it could just be a big coincidence. Then again, a mole's eyesight is pretty lousy, since they spend all of their time crawling around underground where it's dark. So chances were that she hadn't taken a good look at this trigger-happy homeowner at all and was simply making things up. Still, it didn't hurt to check it out. Jackie was obviously a clever mole, and right now she was the only lead we had. "So where was this?"

CHAPTER 18

Odelia was waiting impatiently in the hospital waiting room for news on her husband's condition. It was taking the doctors longer than she had anticipated, and by the time her mom and dad arrived, she still didn't know what was going on and had pretty much been reduced to a nervous wreck.

"I'll see if I can find out more," her dad said, and went in search of one of his colleagues.

Mom took a seat next to her on one of the particularly uncomfortable plastic seats, and took her hand in hers and gave it a squeeze. "He'll be fine," she said. "Chase is young and strong. I'm sure he'll be fine."

"I don't know, Mom," said Odelia, trying to fight tears from spilling down her cheeks. "You should have seen him in that ambulance. He looked so pale and helpless. Almost as if… as if he had already died."

"He's not dead," Mom insisted. "He just had a bad reaction to that prawn, that's all. They'll probably have to pump his stomach or something, and he'll be all right."

"I'm not so sure," she murmured. The paramedics hadn't

told her anything in that ambulance, but they had looked very serious, transmitting the message that Chase's condition was grave. "What if Dad gave him the wrong medicine?" she asked. "What if Chase dies and it turns out that it was Dad's fault?" It was a question she knew she shouldn't be asking, but she couldn't help herself. So many thoughts were going through her mind, and she had to tell someone.

"I'm sure Tex didn't give him the wrong medicine," said Mom. "You know what a good and conscientious doctor your father is, honey. He would never make such a mistake. He just wouldn't."

But it seemed to Odelia that her mom was trying to convince herself first and foremost.

Dad finally returned, holding two cups of coffee, one for his daughter and one for his wife, and shook his head. "I can't seem to be able to get a hold of anyone," he said. "There are a lot of emergencies, apparently, and the ICU is running at full capacity. I guess we'll just have to wait."

"But he is being taken care of, right?" said Odelia, panicking.

"I'm sure he is," her dad said, taking a seat on her other side. "And I'm sure he'll pull through, honey. He's young and strong and—"

"Please don't keep telling me how young and strong he is," said Odelia. "All I want is for someone to tell me that he'll be fine."

"He'll be fine," said her dad after a pause, but somehow his voice lacked the ring of conviction. As if he didn't believe his own words.

"Where is Grace?" asked Odelia suddenly.

"She's with your grandmother," said Mom.

"Good," said Odelia. "What about Francine? Is she all alone in the house?"

"Your gran is with her," said Mom. "She'll keep an eye on things."

"It's not that. She told me she's in danger. She was being followed by some dangerous people. If they find out where she is…" She gulped. If Francine's whereabouts were discovered by these dangerous people, and they attacked her… She took her phone from her pocket.

"Who are you calling?" asked Mom.

"Uncle Alec. If Francine is attacked, with Gran and Grace present…"

"Oh, dear," said Mom.

"Exactly."

She put in the call, and told her uncle about Francine and the people who were supposedly gunning for her. She also told him about Chase, since nobody seemed to have taken the trouble to fill him in.

"Chase is in a coma?!" her uncle cried. "How did that happen!"

"A bad prawn," she said. "At least that's all we know right now."

"Can a bad prawn put you in a coma?" asked her uncle, sounding incredulous. "I ate prawns last night, and so did Charlene."

"We all ate prawns last night," she reminded him.

"What hospital is he in?" he asked. "I'm coming over."

"Better go to the house," she countered. "Make sure Francine is all right, and Gran and Grace."

"I'll send an officer," he said. "I'll send two if you want, or even a dozen. But right now I'm coming over to see my godson, Odelia."

She smiled. "Of course." At least if there was a police presence at the house, no one would dare come anywhere near them. Suddenly an idea struck her. "You don't think the people that are out to hurt Francine could be behind what happened to Chase, do you?"

"Why, did you notice anyone hanging around the house last night?"

"No, I didn't. But one of the reasons Francine chose me is probably because of Chase. She must have figured that with a cop in the house she would be safe. So what if these people somehow found out where she is staying, and they decided to get rid of Chase, to have better access to her?"

"I don't see how they could have managed."

"He was at the station all day yesterday. Could someone have spiked his coffee maybe? Or served him a poisoned donut?"

"I doubt it. If someone had been lurking around the precinct yesterday, I think we would have noticed. And we get our donuts from the same baker who's been serving us for years. Also, if those donuts were poisoned, the entire station would be in a coma right now. Same thing for the coffee."

"I guess so," she said, her shoulders sagging again.

"I'll definitely look into it, though. Do they know what's wrong with him yet?"

"Not yet. Dad says the ICU is being overrun with patients right now, so it might be a while before they are able to tell us something."

"How are you holding up?"

"I'm holding up."

"Good girl."

She disconnected, and for a while the three of them sat there, staring before them and wishing for a happy ending. Then Mom suddenly dug into her purse and took out a plastic baggie.

"What's that?" asked Odelia.

"Prawns," said Mom with a note of triumph.

CHAPTER 19

"You're not supposed to lick it, Brutus," Harriet said.

"But it itches!" her partner lamented.

"I know," she said, softening. With her it also itched, and she was having just as hard a time not licking the injured spots. But if she wanted her perfectly groomed fur to stay as pristinely white as it had always been, this was a sacrifice she had to make. So in spite of the temptation to apply her raspy tongue to the itchy spots, she had refrained from going against Vena's strict instructions.

"How long do you think it will take to get rid of this thing?" asked Brutus.

They were in Marge and Tex's backyard, relaxing underneath the rose bushes, their favorite spot.

"I have no idea," she admitted. "But I don't think it will be long. Otherwise Vena would have said."

"You know, I think I'll have to revise my view on vets in general and Vena in particular. She does seem to have her uses."

"She does," Harriet admitted. Loath as she was to give

credit to the woman she had always viewed as a butcher of the most vicious kind, she had to admit she seemed to know what she was doing.

"I'll bet they'll get us to stay out here until we're cured," said Brutus moodily. "Well, if that happens I'm out of here, sweetie pie."

"They're allowing us the use of the downstairs floor," Harriet said, reminding her mate of Marge's words. "Provided we don't go anywhere near any of them."

"Mh," Brutus grumbled.

"And look at the bright side: they'll clean the whole house with bleach. That's nice, isn't it? I happen to like the smell of bleach."

"Who doesn't? Bleach just may be the best invention man made since he discovered the wheel. But she shouldn't have said that thing about staying away from them, sugar plum. That wasn't very nice."

"Look at it from their point of view: they don't want to get the same stuff on them we got on us." She still blamed Clarice, or Shanille, and was determined to get to the bottom of who had transferred this horrible fungus to her precious person.

"I guess," he said reluctantly.

They mused on their situation, heads on their front paws, and generally enjoying each other's company, when suddenly they saw a man appear they had never seen before. He was dressed in a tracksuit, like the ones Gran liked to wear, and was behaving very suspiciously indeed.

"Who's that?" she asked, gesturing toward the newcomer.

"No idea. Maybe a friend of Marge and Tex?"

"I doubt it. We know all of their friends, and I've never seen this guy before."

"Maybe he's one of Marge's customers at the library and he's returning a book after hours?"

The man was checking the back of the house, looking it up and down, with a particular interest in the upstairs windows, one of which was open in the tilt position.

"What's that bulge in his pants?" asked Brutus.

The man did indeed have a noticeable bulge at the back of his pants. The shape looked familiar as well. He had approached the kitchen, and tried the handle by rattling it for a moment.

"Where is Gran?" asked Harriet.

"Out," said Brutus. "She went for a walk with Grace."

"Good thing she locked the door before she left."

The man was glancing up at that window again, and seemed to have an idea. He now approached the garden house, to the side of which a ladder had been attached. He grabbed the ladder from the hooks on which it rested and took it up to the house, then placed it against the facade.

"I think it's a burglar, sweetie," said Brutus.

"I think you're right," said Harriet. "And that bulge in his pants is probably a gun." The man's jacket was riding up as he climbed the ladder, and she could see a glint of cold hard steel sticking out of his back pants pocket.

"This isn't good," said Brutus.

"We should do something."

Brutus gulped audibly. "Where is Max when you need him?"

"He's right next door, sugar pie. He's talking to that mole."

"Let's go fetch him. Maybe he's got some bright idea."

And so it was decided. They snuck from underneath the rose bushes, crawled across the lawn in the direction of the hedge, and disappeared through the opening, their eyes never leaving the burglar.

They found Max and Dooley in the backyard, chatting amiably with the mole. Strictly speaking they were trespassing, since Francine had told them in no uncertain terms she wasn't going to allow them access to either the house or the backyard. But since Francine was nowhere in sight, the point was moot.

"Max!" Brutus hissed, careful not to raise his voice, lest the burglar would hear them. "There's a burglar breaking into the house next door."

"And he's got a gun!" Harriet added.

Max seemed startled by this piece of news. "A burglar with a gun? Are you sure?"

"No, I'm kidding," said Brutus with an eye roll. "Of course I'm sure! He took the ladder and he's trying to get into Gran's room."

"Where is Gran?" asked Max. "And Grace?"

"Gone for a walk around the block," said Harriet.

"Right," said Max, thinking this through. Harriet could practically see the little cogs and wheels in that big brain of his moving.

"Shall I bite him in the ankles, Max?" Dooley suggested.

"It's a possibility," Max said. "And if he wasn't carrying a gun, I would strongly advocate it. We need to be careful, though."

"We're no match for a gun," said Brutus.

That was an understatement. If it hadn't been for that gun, they could have handled that burglar all by themselves. No need to trouble Max. Right now only their friend's brainpower could thwart this burglar.

CHAPTER 20

It certainly was a tough nut to crack, I thought. But then I remembered that burglars are notoriously timid people. They don't like to be seen, and prefer to carry out their burglarious activities undetected. Which is how I got the idea to try a little experiment.

"How is your singing voice, Harriet?" I asked.

Harriet gave me an odd look. "Excellent, as always," she said. "Why?"

"I want you to go next door and sing," I said.

"What do you mean?"

"Can you please trust me?" I said. "Just go back and sing."

"Music soothes the savage beast," Brutus commented. "Is that what you're thinking, Max?"

"That's exactly what I'm thinking," I confirmed.

Brutus turned to his mate. "Your singing will bring tears to the eyes of that burglar and will make him repent, sweet pea. Just you wait and see."

"Oh, Max," said Harriet, perking up immediately. "That's the most brilliant thing I've ever heard! Of course I'll go and sing for that man. Appeal to his better nature."

And so the four of us tripped into Marge and Tex's backyard, followed by Jackie, who was curious to see what would happen when Harriet opened her lungs to their full capacity and gave of her best.

The burglar was trying to jimmy Gran's window, even though I could have told him that his haul would be meager if he succeeded. The Pooles, contrary to some, don't keep large piles of money and jewels and gold in the house, mainly because they don't possess them. But it's hard to argue with a burglar once he's got his eye on you, of course. Better to dissuade him by putting the spotlight on him.

We positioned ourselves at the bottom of that ladder.

"Isn't he going to shoot me?" asked Harriet nervously.

"No, he won't," I assured her. "The moment he hears you sing he'll be so moved he'll simply break down and cry his heart out."

She smiled. "Oh, Max. You're such a clever pussycat." Then she filled her lungs with some much-needed oxygen and struck the first note of Celine Dion's *My Heart Will Go On*, one of her favorite songs of all time.

The effect on the burglar was immediate. A visible tremor shook him from stem to stern, and for a moment I thought he was going to fall down from that ladder. But he clung to it for dear life even as Harriet's caterwauling washed over him and played on his eardrums like a chainsaw on a piece of plywood.

Harriet may not be the best singer in the world, but what she lacks in talent she makes up for in sheer volume. She can belt out a tune like no one else I know.

The burglar, having searched around for the source of the sound, which somehow reminded me of nails dragging across a blackboard, now looked down, and when he saw the four of us, started violently.

"Okay, you guys," I said. "Let's give Harriet some backing

vocals." And so we all opened our pipes and joined in. Even Jackie decided to add her own voice to the chorus and produced some gentle squeaking sounds. All in all I think we did a pretty great job, considering our audience existed of only the one person.

But that was about to change.

"What's with the racket!" suddenly an irate voice sounded.

I smiled, for I had recognized the voice as belonging to Odelia's next-door neighbor Kurt Mayfield. The man is a retired music teacher, and our singing seems to offend his professional taste.

He now came charging through the hedge, and when he saw that burglar clinging to that ladder, his jaw dropped a couple of inches.

"What in the name of…" he said. "Hey, you!" he added, shaking an irate fist. "Get down from there at once!"

The burglar didn't need to be told twice. In fact I don't think I've ever seen a man move as fast as he did. Using a fireman's slide he was down that ladder in milliseconds, then he was racing for the fence located at the back of the garden, hopped over it like a jackrabbit and was gone.

"And stay out!" Kurt yelled.

"I think we better stop now," I told the others as Kurt approached with a dangerous gleam in his eye.

But of course I should have known it's a lot harder to get Harriet to stop singing than it is to get her to begin. So even though Brutus, Dooley and I—and Jackie—abruptly downed tools, Harriet kept on screeching out her favorite song. I could tell she was working up to the chorus, her favorite part.

It was at this point that Kurt grabbed her by the neck and picked her up. "I told you to stop," he said quietly, but with menace.

The song was turned off with a final squeak, and she stared into the man's eyes, transfixed.

Then suddenly his usually implacable face morphed into a grin. "You got rid of that burglar, didn't you? Very clever, Harriet. Very clever indeed." And then he set her down again, and left the backyard, whistling a pleasant tune.

"I didn't even know he knew my name," said Harriet, much impressed.

"Who was that?" asked Jackie.

"Our neighbor Kurt Mayfield," I said. "He doesn't like it when we sing."

"Which you were banking on," said Brutus with a grin. "Clever, Max. Very clever."

It wasn't the final surprise of the day, for moments later Kurt came walking back through that same hedge, only this time he had two police officers in tow. And he proceeded to explain to them where he had seen the burglar, and where the man had escaped to. Immediately they went in pursuit of the miscreant.

Arriving home from her walk at that exact moment, Gran entered the backyard. "What are you doing here?" she asked Kurt. She was carrying Grace in her arms, and the latter looked very pleased with herself.

"We went for a nice walk," Grace told us. "And I even got an ice cream."

"Good for you," I said wholeheartedly, since I know how much Grace adores ice cream.

"I caught a burglar," Kurt explained. "He was up that ladder when I arrived," he said, pointing to the window of Gran's room. "And trying to break into that window over there."

"Hey, but that's my room!" said Gran.

"Yeah, well, the cats were screaming and making that godawful noise they always make, so I decided to see what they were up to. Which is when I came face to face with that burglar. The moment I set foot in here he skedaddled. And so I called the cops. Only turns out they were already here, watching the house for some reason, and when I told them about the burglar, they went after him. I doubt they'll catch him, though. He was fast."

"He was fast," I confirmed.

"What's a burglar, Max?" asked Grace.

"Well, a burglar is a person who breaks into places where he doesn't live to steal things that don't belong to him," I said.

"That's not a very nice thing to do," she said.

"No, it's not very nice indeed," I confirmed.

I saw that the front of her shirt was full of ice cream, which told me that probably half of the stuff had ended up in her tummy and the other on her T-shirt. But she didn't seem to mind one bit.

"I wonder what he was doing here," said Gran. "I mean, there isn't anything worth stealing."

"They're just looking," said Kurt. "Checking out places and hoping to find something. And there's always something, Vesta. I mean, you own a TV, right? And probably a phone, maybe a computer? That's enough to make it worth their while."

"I guess so," said Gran.

"What's all this I hear about Chase being taken to the hospital?" asked Kurt. "Is he going to be all right?"

"I don't know," said Gran. "He's in a coma, and we don't know why. So it's up to the doctors to come up with answers. Marge and Tex and Odelia are at the hospital. They left me here to take care of Grace."

"I hope he's fine," said Kurt. "He's a great guy, Chase is, and a great neighbor." He smiled. "But then you're all great neighbors, Vesta. I really lucked out in that department."

He took his leave, with Gran staring after him. Once

again he was whistling a little tune, and looking for all intents and purposes like a man in love with life.

And then I remembered. Kurt had recently become engaged to the lady who lived next door from him. Gilda Goldstein and Kurt had even celebrated Christmas together, and might be moving in together.

"He's changed his tune," said Gran now.

"Kurt is in love," I said.

"Oh, that's right. I forgot about that. Well, good for him."

And good for us, his lucky neighbors.

The two cops now came crawling over the fence again. They both looked slightly out of breath.

"And? Did you catch the guy?" asked Gran.

"Catch the burglar!" Grace cried.

"He got away," said the largest of the two. He stood with his hands on his knees, panting and trying to catch his breath.

"We got a glimpse of the getaway car, though," said the second cop, who was skinny and in much better shape than his colleague. "Black sedan. I even got a plate," he added triumphantly, and held up his phone.

"You got a picture?" asked his colleague. "Show us, will you?"

Gran and the large cop joined to look at the skinny cop's phone.

"And bingo!" said the skinny cop. "Perfect snap!"

"Probably a fake plate," said his colleague.

"We'll know soon enough."

"You guys want to come in?" said Gran.

"No, that's all right, Vesta," said the largest cop. "Alec told us to keep an eye out for intruders, so we need to get back to our post."

"I'll bring you a nice cup of coffee," said Gran. "And cake."

The smiles on the faces of the two cops spoke volumes.

CHAPTER 21

Francine had been vaguely aware of some kind of commotion next door, but it was only when first a large man traipsed through the garden, followed by two cops, that she understood that something was seriously amiss. It didn't take long for her to put two and two together, and when Odelia's grandmother told her that the police had almost caught a burglar trying to get into the house, she knew.

That wasn't a burglar, you silly woman, she thought. That was one of the men trying to get to me!

They had been following her that morning, and even though she was sure she had been able to shake them off before she set foot in Odelia's office, now she wasn't so sure anymore. Had they managed to find out where she was staying? If that was the case, she wasn't safe anymore. Then again, if they knew the police were watching the house, as Mrs. Muffin had told her, they might use their heads and stay away.

"Who ordered the police to watch the house?" she asked.

She and Mrs. Muffin were chatting in the backyard of the

woman's home, where apparently this burglar had appeared, then skedaddled.

"My granddaughter. She's at the hospital with her husband, and so is my daughter and son-in-law. So they were worried that you were alone in the house. So she asked my son, who's the chief of police, to watch the house and make sure you were safe."

She breathed a sigh of relief. "That was very thoughtful of her."

"Odelia is like that. She always puts others first."

"Yes, I was surprised when she agreed to put me up for a while," said Francine. Most people she knew would never have said yes, but Odelia didn't have to think twice. She felt a little bad about the woman's husband, though. "Is Chase going to be all right?"

"We're not sure yet," said Mrs. Muffin. "We're still waiting on the results from the tests they're running. We thought it was a bad prawn, but now we're not so sure."

"Can eating a bad prawn put you in a coma?"

"I'd be very surprised if it did," Mrs. Muffin said.

"Well, Mrs. Muffin, I want to thank you for telling me all of this. I was wondering what was going on when I heard all the noise."

"It's Vesta, and you don't have to thank me, honey. It's all part of the service." The old lady gave her a smile that warmed Francine's heart. They really were nice people. Too bad she had to deceive them.

"There's one thing I did notice," she said. "And that's your cats. They were in the backyard again. Now I know I'm being a pain in the ass here, but would it be possible to—"

"I'll make sure they don't bother you again," Vesta said.

"Thank you," she said. "It's just that I'm afraid I'm allergic to the creatures. I didn't think I was, but every time they come anywhere near me I get a runny nose and I start sneezing like crazy."

"Say no more," said the old lady, holding up a hand. "I understand perfectly. And besides, now that they've been diagnosed with ringworm, it's probably best if you stay away from them."

"Ringworm!"

"Yeah, can you imagine? They must have picked it up from one of their friends. They move around a lot, you know, especially at night. And who knows where they go, right?"

Francine shivered. Ringworm. Yuck. "You should probably clean the house," she said. "And wash all the clothes, beddings, towels—everything they could have been in contact with."

"Yeah, I know the drill," said Vesta. "But with Chase in hospital, and me taking care of the little one…"

"Why don't I take care of your granddaughter's house?" she suggested.

Vesta's eyebrows shot up into her little white curls. "You want to clean Odelia's house?"

"Absolutely. It's the least I can do in return for her hospitality." And that way she would make doubly sure the house was devoid of any of that horrible fungus.

"Well, that would be swell. I'd do it myself, but I'm a little busy, as you can probably imagine."

"Don't you give it a second thought. I'll take care of everything. And by the time Odelia returns with her husband, they'll find the place spic and span."

The smile the lady bestowed on her was something to behold.

And she had just returned to the backyard of the house she now considered her temporary home, when she noticed something small and brown slithering between her feet, then skitter away and disappear into one of those unsightly molehills that littered the place. Her face took on a set expression. The fungus wasn't the only vermin she had to eradicate. Clearly Odelia had a mole problem. But not for long. Once she was done with the house, she would take care of the garden. And get rid of that mole once and for all.

* * *

KEVIN ROBINSON, known to his friends as Kev, had put the pedal to the metal and managed to get out of town at a speed that probably couldn't be considered healthy—or indeed legal. But he had to get out of there as fast as he could. The last thing he needed right now was for the cops to arrest him and haul him to prison.

He arrived at the old farmhouse where he and his partner had set up their temporary headquarters and parked the car behind it, then pulled a large tarpaulin over it, just to be safe.

He entered the main house and discovered that while he was away, Steve had put his feet up and was watching television.

"What did I tell you?" he asked, kicking Steve's feet from the chair. "No TV on the job, Steve. We can't afford to get distracted."

"There's nothing else to do around here!" said Steve, who was a heavyset man with a ponytail and a large bald spot on top of his head.

Steve had a point, of course. There wasn't a lot to do around the place, except watch television.

"How did it go? Did you find her?"

"I found her all right, but before I could get in, some big dude almost grabbed me." He didn't mention he'd checked out the wrong house, something he only realized when he was on his way back to the farm.

"Who grabbed you?" asked Steve, sitting up with a jerk.

"I didn't stick around long enough to find out," he said, raking a hand through his curly mane. "But when I was making my way back to the car, I could have sworn I was being chased by two cops." They got there so fast they must have been watching the house. Which told him Francine Martin must have been right next door. It would make their job a lot harder, of course, but that couldn't be helped.

"You have to be more careful, Kev," said his partner in crime. "If they catch you, it's game over."

"I know that," he said irritably. "You don't have to tell me how to do my job."

"Looks like I do. At least the intel panned out, correct?"

"Correct," he confirmed. Though he hadn't actually clapped eyes on the target, he knew he'd come close. If only those cops hadn't been there… And those darn cats, of course, with their infernal racket.

He wondered if the cops would watch the house day and night. Presumably they would, which meant Miss Martin was off limits for now. But at least he knew where she was holed up, which was better than having her out there in the wild, busy doing who knows what.

"So now what?" asked Steve.

"Now we wait until she makes her next move."

"To do that we need to have eyes on the target, Kev."

"I know. And I know exactly how to make sure we do."

CHAPTER 22

Mike was concerned when Francine told him what had happened. "A burglar? Are you all right?"

"Yeah, one of the neighbors saw him and he ran. Then the police got involved, but they didn't catch him."

"And you don't think this was a coincidence?"

"Pretty sure he was after one thing and one thing only."

"The diary. So is it safe?"

"You don't think I'd be stupid enough to keep it on me, do you? Yeah, it's safe, all right. Safe where no burglar will be able to get it."

"Thank God. You should make copies, Francine. Imagine if something happens to the original. We'd be sunk."

"Oh, I made copies. Don't you worry about that."

Mike gazed out the window of his office, which offered a view of the long driveway that led to the road. Emily and her mom had gone to Manhattan to go shopping, and wouldn't be back until tomorrow, which meant he had the place to himself. Not that he was all that keen on being alone. Contrary to what he had always assumed he was actually a family man, and never happier than in the company of his wife and daughter. But he had to admit that it was easier to get things done when it was just him, and Yvonne and Em weren't there to grab his attention, as they invariably did.

His big Dalmatian Bruno had traipsed up to him and now pressed his nose against the back of his hand. "Okay, so I've talked to the lawyers, and they reckon we stand a pretty good chance to have the deal nullified after all. Certain provisions in the original contract seem to make it feasible to get out. There will be damages, of course, but nothing we can't handle, provided that mine is as rich as you say it is."

"I'm not the one saying it, Mike. Our great-grandfather is."

He patted Bruno's head affectionately. "So here's what we'll do. We'll get together here at the house, you and me, and we'll both bring something to the table this time. You'll provide the diary, and allow my expert to take a closer look at the thing and determine its authenticity. And I'll bring an ironclad contract that we will both sign, giving us equal rights to the proceeds of the mine. How does that sound?"

"You're sure you can get out of that original contract?"

"My lawyers are talking to their lawyers, but so far the feedback is positive. As long as they don't know the real reason we're reneging on the deal, no harm done. Of course if word got out about the lithium, that would be a different matter altogether. So it's important you don't tell a living, breathing soul about this."

"And the same goes for you, cousin."

He smiled. "Agreed. So how about it, Francine? Ready to cross that bridge and make things official? I know it's a big step but it's important I get a good look at that diary before I sign anything."

"Agreed," she said. "So when do you want to do this?"

"As soon as possible." As he talked to her, he'd become

aware of some strange background sounds on her end. He asked now, "What is that sound? Almost as if someone is scrubbing something."

"That's me. I'm cleaning the house. The cats here have ringworm, and I volunteered to disinfect the place with bleach."

He couldn't imagine his glamorous cousin on hands and knees scrubbing the floor, so he laughed. "You've got to be kidding me."

"They're providing me with security and a place to stay, Mike, so it's the least I can do to repay them for their kindness."

"Well, all right. I'll set up the meeting. How does tomorrow morning at ten o'clock sound to you?"

"Sounds fine to me. It's just that..." She hesitated.

"What is it?"

"Remember I told you I was followed after our last meeting? I have a hunch it's the same guy who tried to break into the house next door. They probably got some wrong intel, or maybe they bungled the job. So I don't feel entirely safe anymore, Mike."

"You should come and stay here at the mansion," he said. "I've got plenty of security. You'll be perfectly safe, you know that, Francine."

"Yeah, I know, but people will start to ask questions."

"What people? The only ones who'll know you're here is my family and me. And they won't talk to anyone."

"You don't know that. People talk, Mike."

"Not if I tell them not to."

"You're going to tell your daughter not to tell anyone your cousin is staying with you? Get real, Mike. She's a kid. The first thing she'll do is tell all of her friends. Or she'll make a TikTok video or an Instagram post or whatever it is that kids do nowadays. And next thing you know the whole world will know."

It was true, of course. The moment he told Emily, she would probably do exactly what he told her not to do. Even Yvonne couldn't be counted on to keep Francine's presence at the mansion a secret.

"Okay, so what do you suggest?"

"Odelia's uncle arranged for a police presence at the house, so I'm safe as long as I stay here. But I can hardly ask them to give me a police escort when I go meet with you tomorrow morning, can I?"

He nodded. "I'll send a car round to pick you up. Just text me the address."

"Will do," she said. "Oh, and Mike?"

"What?"

"Send plenty of muscle, will you? I have a feeling these people mean business. And if they can grab me, they won't hesitate."

CHAPTER 23

After having sat there for what felt like hours, the doctor in charge of Chase's hospitalization finally joined them in the waiting room. Presently he invited them into his office, and when Odelia's mom and dad got up to follow him, he told her, "Just you for now, Odelia."

She exchanged a look of surprise with her mom, but followed the doctor into a small office. She didn't know the man very well, but she had met him once or twice, and knew he was a consummate professional. Doctor Reynolds had been one of several people she had interviewed when she was doing a piece on Hampton Cove Memorial Hospital a while ago, and she remembered him as a man who didn't mince words.

He didn't do so now.

"Your husband was drugged, Odelia."

Whatever she had expected, it wasn't this. "Drugged? What do you mean?"

"We found GHB in his system, and plenty of it. Enough to knock him out for several hours."

"GHB? You mean—"

"The date rape drug, yes. Do you have any idea how he might have gotten it into his system?"

She blinked as she tried to imagine Chase being drugged. Or Chase taking drugs? No. No way. He wasn't into that sort of thing. And besides, if he was taking drugs she would know about it. She would have noticed. Wouldn't she? "I have no idea," she said finally.

Doctor Reynolds leaned back. "GHB, or Gamma-Hydroxybutyrate, is usually taken in liquid form. Either ingested or injected, though mostly the former. It's sold in vials and often added to fruit juice, alcohol or plain water. It's odorless and almost tasteless. And when you take too much of the stuff, as your husband did, it can be lethal."

"How much did he take?"

The doctor grimaced. "Enough to put him in a coma."

"Will he—"

"Survive? Yes, he will. We're monitoring him closely and expect him to make a full recovery."

"But where did it come from? I mean, he spent all day yesterday at the office, then last night we had dinner—prawns."

"Yes, those famous prawns," said the doctor. "Your mother submitted the remnants of your dinner and we're having it tested, but I very much doubt those prawns had anything to do with what happened to your husband, Odelia."

"What about the sleeping pill my dad gave him?" she asked, and was afraid to hear the answer.

"Zolpidem, yes. In and of itself there's nothing harmful about it. It's a relatively mild sedative, used for remedying short-term sleeping difficulties. But in combination with the GHB… Lucky for Chase he only took a small dose. If he had taken more he might not be able to tell the tale, I'm afraid."

"Oh, God."

"Look, in cases like these we normally inform the police. So I've taken the liberty of calling your uncle, and he was as surprised as you are that we found drugs in Chase's system. He says he can vouch for his detective and insists he must be the victim of a crime. So they're sending someone around to take Chase's statement as soon as he's conscious. I just thought you would want to be informed of the proceedings."

"Thank you, doctor," she said gratefully.

"Let's hope they can find out how he was drugged," said the doctor as he got up from behind the desk. "And make sure it doesn't happen again. Cause next time he might not be so lucky." He gave her a look of significance, to show her he wasn't kidding.

She nodded wearily. "When can I see him?"

"As soon as he wakes up," the doctor assured her. "Which I expect will be at some point during the night. So if you want to go home and rest, I can have someone call you as soon as there's a change in his condition."

"No, I'll stay here," she said decidedly. "I want to be there when he wakes up."

"That's fine," he said warmly, and let her out.

She joined her parents, who were understandably anxious. When she told them they had found GHB in Chase's system, her dad paled considerably. "Oh, no," he said, bringing a distraught hand to his face. "And I gave him Zolpidem. I could have killed him!"

"Yeah, Doctor Reynolds said the combination is potentially lethal. But he also said he only ingested a small dose of the sleeping pill, so it should be fine."

"Still," said Dad, looking as if he was about to pass out. "If only I'd known about the GHB, I would never have given him that pill."

"You couldn't possibly have known, honey," said Marge, placing her hand on his arm. "Chase probably didn't know it himself. Did he?" she asked, directing an anxious look at her daughter.

Odelia knew exactly what that look meant: had her husband knowingly and consciously ingested that drug? In other words: was Chase a drug addict? It happened all the time, even in the best of families, that a spouse or a child was secretly an addict. Some of them were very clever about hiding their addiction, making sure no one found out. Until someone gave them half a sleeping pill and it put them in a coma because of the effect of the combination of drugs.

"That's for Uncle Alec to find out," she said. She liked to think that she would have noticed if her husband was an addict, but she was smart enough to realize that she simply had no way of knowing. It was true that in his line of work Chase got in touch with all kinds of people, the most unsavory first. If he wanted to, he could easily have had access to the stuff. So had he succumbed to the temptation?

But then her phone chimed and she saw that her grandmother was trying to reach her. She picked up immediately. "Gran, good news," she said. "Chase will make a full recovery."

"Oh, honey, that's wonderful news," said her grandmother. "But I'm afraid news from home is a little less uplifting." And as Gran told her about the burglar they almost caught, Odelia closed her eyes. What was happening? First Chase, then the cats getting infected, and now burglars trying to break into Mom and Dad's house.

"So he got away?"

"Yeah, he did, but one of your uncle's officers snapped a picture of the license plate, so they're going to run it through their system and hopefully will come up with a match."

"At least that's something." Though she knew from experience these people usually used false plates when they were on a job. So chances were that nothing would come of this. Still, the burglar hadn't been able to take anything, so there was that.

"Are you coming home?" asked Gran.

"No, I'm going to wait until Chase wakes up. But Mom and Dad will probably be home." She directed a questioning look at her mom, who was rubbing Dad's shoulder. Mom nodded. "Yeah, they'll be home, so you're relieved from babysitting duties, Gran."

"Oh, I don't mind. Grace is the sweetest girl in the world. I treated her to some ice cream this afternoon. I hope you don't mind."

She smiled. "No, that's fine." Gran was really spoiling her. But then that was probably what grandparents were for, and great-grandparents even more.

"Did you know it was actually the cats that managed to scare off that burglar? Max's idea. He got Harriet to sing a serenade to the burglar, which got Kurt so upset he came stomping over. The burglar took one look at Kurt and took off like a bat out of hell. At which point Kurt called the police, who were already sitting in a patrol car in front of the house, and they chased the burglar all the way to the next street."

"Clever Max," said Odelia.

"He is. Okay, I gotta run. I've got something on the stove for Grace. Oh, and your guest has kindly offered to clean your house with bleach. Top to bottom. As a token of her appreciation."

"Tell her I said thanks."

"Give my love to Chase when he wakes up."

"I will."

She hung up and tapped the phone against her chin. "A burglar tried to break into the house," she told her parents. "But the cats and Kurt managed to chase him off."

Marge shook her head. "What is happening!"

Her sentiments exactly.

CHAPTER 24

Grace had been studying the cats for a while now. She was safely hidden inside the house while the feline contingent stayed outside, so they wouldn't get into any contact with her. As far as she could tell there was nothing physically wrong with them, in spite of her great-grandmother's word of warning not to get too close to them and above all: never to touch them under any circumstance!

She liked touching the cats. They were soft and warm and made a pleasant purring sound when touched with kindness. And now she wasn't allowed to touch them anymore? And all because of something called a fungus. She didn't even know what a fungus was, but it didn't sound all that horrible.

She'd seen cartoons about the most monstrous villains, and none of them had ever referred to a fungus as their newest super weapon with which they were going to destroy the planet. So she really didn't see the point of steering clear of her dear, dear friends.

And so when Max crept into the kitchen through the pet flap on his way to his litter box, she cried with joy. "Max!"

she yelled when she caught sight of the voluminous orange kitty. "Let's play a game!"

Max grimaced. "I'm afraid we're not allowed to play with you, honey," he said. "We're suffering from some kind of disease, you see, which is very contagious. And we don't want you to get it, too. So you better stay far away from us, you hear?"

"But I don't want to stay far away from you!" she insisted. "I want to hug you and I want to pet you and I want to give you a big kiss on top of your head."

"You can't do any of those things, Gracie," said Max, a note of alarm in his voice. "So please respect the boundaries. As soon as we're better you can hug us again, but not until Gran gives you the green light, is that understood?"

A second cat entered through the pet flap. It was Dooley, and when he caught sight of her he stiffened. "Grace!" he said with a touch of awkwardness. "What are you doing here? I thought you were upstairs."

"I'm not upstairs. I got bored upstairs. I want to play with you guys."

"But you can't," said Dooley. "You can't come anywhere near us."

More cats poured in through the pet flap, namely Harriet and Brutus. Now all four cats stood staring at her with some concern.

"I thought you were my friends," she said. "And now you're telling me I can't even kiss you? That's not fair!"

"Life isn't fair," Brutus grumbled. "Deal with it."

"Brutus, that's no way to talk to the kid," said Harriet.

"It's time someone told her some hard truths," Brutus said. "She has to learn sometime so why not now?" He turned to her. "Life is full of disappointments and heartache, toots. You simply gotta learn to roll with the punches."

"Roll with the punches?" asked Grace. "What do you mean, Brutus?"

"Well..."

"See what you did?" said Harriet. "Now she's all confused. I told you not to talk to her like that."

"I think what Brutus means to say," said Dooley, "is that you can't always get what you want in life, and that's all right. You simply have to accept and move on. It's a lesson I learned from Max. You see, Max always wanted to be an athletic cat, just like Brutus. Only his body type isn't made for that kind of thing. And so Max has had to accept that he will never be as slim and as athletic and as handsome as Brutus."

Brutus was laughing loudly at this. "I like your explanation, Dooley. In fact I love it. Very apt."

"But it's all right," Dooley continued. "Because Max has something that Brutus doesn't have. You see, Max is very clever, and Brutus isn't. Brutus may be handsome and strong and a great athlete, but he's also a little stupid, and that's fine."

Brutus wasn't laughing anymore. Instead he was growling softly, making menacing noises that didn't sound all that nice. Meanwhile Max was grinning. He seemed to enjoy Dooley's speech tremendously.

"And what about me, Dooley?" asked Harriet. "What hardships did I have to overcome to get where I am today?"

"Well, Harriet is very pretty," said Dooley. "But unfortunately she's also a little mean. She's a diva, you see, and divas may be popular, and they may be admired by everybody, but they're also self-centered and selfish. They only think about themselves, and not about others, which makes them very unlikable. But that's fine, because they're so talented and so beautiful that people forgive them these foibles."

"Foibles," Max murmured. "Hilarious."

Harriet shot Max a look that could kill, but the big cat took it in stride.

"So what about you, Dooley?" asked Grace.

"Me?" Dooley seemed surprised. "You want to know about me?"

"That's right. What's the good and the bad about you?"

"Well..." He glanced around uncertainly. "That's not for me to say, Grace. I think others will be better placed to make that judgment. Max?"

Max cleared his throat. "There's nothing bad about Dooley. In fact Dooley can only be described as the perfect friend and the best cat that I ever had the pleasure of knowing. In other words: Dooley is fine."

"And what about me?" asked Grace.

Four cats stared at her in wonder. Then they all smiled in unison. "You're fine, too," said Max finally. "Nothing wrong with you, kiddo."

"And I think you're all swell," said Grace happily. Even though she couldn't touch the cats, she could talk to them, and for now that would have to do.

Moments later Granny came walking into the kitchen, and cried, "Didn't I tell you to stay away from Grace? Jesus! Out!"

"But Gran," Dooley said. "I have to tinkle!"

"Then tinkle, and don't dawdle. The rest of you: out!"

But as it transpired, all of the cats had to tinkle, and Brutus's expression told Grace that he might have to do something more. And so Granny ushered Grace out of the kitchen and into the living room, where she was safe from the dreadful fungus the cats were apparently carrying.

"I know it's hard to stay away, Gracie," said Granny, wagging a reproachful finger. "But it's for your own good, you understand? And now be a good girl and stay here, all right?"

And then she resumed her cleaning efforts. She was planning to clean the entire house with bleach, which smelled nice but was a big job for such an old lady. Soon Gran would come, Granny had told her, so she could help her clean the house. Right now she was at the hospital, where they had taken Daddy, who was sick. But very soon they would all be home again: Mommy, Daddy, Gran, Granddad and Granny. The whole family, in fact. She couldn't wait.

CHAPTER 25

The preparations for the show jumping competition were in full swing, and Sylvia, from her vantage point at the edge of the arena, had an excellent view of Emily and Fury as they made their way around the course. The idea was to get both horse and rider acquainted with the ring and the obstacles, to learn where the judges would be located, and anything else that was pertinent. Next to Sylvie, Emily's mother stood, and Sylvie could sense that she was actually more nervous than her daughter, or the horse for that matter.

They had a lot riding on this, of course, since Sylvie knew they had told Emily's dad that they were going shopping for the weekend in New York, when instead they were out here in Westchester County, getting ready for Emily's very first equestrian jumping event. The Westchester Horse Show welcomed participants of all ages, though Em would compete in the twelve-to-fourteen category, which she had qualified for only a month before. She'd been looking forward to this for a long time, and had been working hard with Fury to get ready for her first show jumping competition. If things went well, they could take home a trophy, and announce the good news to Emily's dad. Even though he wouldn't be happy that they had deceived him, they were all hoping he would be pleased that his daughter had won a prize at her first event, and they were banking on him to be so proud he'd forget to be mad about the fib.

If she lost, or if something happened,... Now, that was a different matter altogether. Stallions like Fury cost an arm and a leg to keep, and if something happened to Emily's horse, Mike would be furious. But if something happened to Emily, he would be devastated. So they had a lot riding on this, something Emily wasn't fully aware of, since her only concern and focus was the competition and finishing first. But her mom knew the stakes better than her daughter, and it showed in the pinched look on her face.

Yvonne was a beautiful woman, with long blond hair just like her daughter, and since Sylvie's mom had died when she was very young, she had always considered Yvonne like a mother to her. For a long time she had even harbored a secret wish that Emily's mom would divorce Mike and marry Sylvie's dad instead. That way she and Em could be sisters and she could live in the big house with her new family. But she had reached an age now where she knew that would never happen. But something else could. Something that would bring her and Emily very close together, and actually create a bond for life.

As things stood, she knew their friendship wouldn't last. Emily was destined for greatness. Whereas Sylvia obviously wasn't. Not in the state she was in. At some point Emily would get bored of spending time with her crippled friend and would dump her in favor of girls like herself: pretty and successful.

She felt her pocket, where she had tucked away her secret

weapon. She hadn't fully decided whether to use it or not. She could always back out.

Next to her, a man had appeared. He looked a little out of place at such a prestigious event. Most of the people there were parents of kids entering the competition, and because of the location of the event it stood to reason that most of them were pretty well-off. But this man looked as if he had slept in his car last night: his pants were creased and a little soiled, his shoes weren't nice and shiny like most people's shoes were, and he was wearing an old fleece sweater that needed a wash—or to be discarded altogether and replaced.

For some reason he was watching Emily and Fury intently, and Sylvie didn't like the look on the man's face. As if he wanted something from Emily.

She glanced up at Yvonne, wondering if she had noticed the same thing. But Emily's mom was too preoccupied to notice anything. Her focus was on her daughter, excluding everything and everyone else—Sylvie included.

She sighed. So she was invisible again. As usual. She wondered why she had agreed to come. To support her friend? But Emily was too busy riding Fury to notice any spectators. In others words: nobody needed her. But that would all change soon.

Tomorrow was the big day. The competition Emily had been talking about for years. Sylvie's hand disappeared into her pocket. Would she use it or not? Right now she was leaning toward yes.

CHAPTER 26

Night had fallen and of my humans there was no sign. The doctors were keeping Chase overnight for observation, and Odelia had told her parents that she would stay at the hospital, in case he woke up. Tex and Marge had arrived home, and had delivered a full report to Gran, who in turn had transmitted the report to us, just to keep us in the loop.

It certainly gave us food for thought. Chase had been poisoned. Or had he suddenly become a drug addict? The opinions were divided on the issue, that much was obvious. Gran seemed to lean toward Chase being a rabid druggie, whereas both Marge and Tex refused to harbor such a terrible thought.

Dooley and I were firmly in their camp, while Brutus and Harriet seemed convinced that the stresses of the job had driven our human to imbibe illegal substances on a regular basis.

"It's only natural that a man in his position would become an addict," Brutus explained as we all sat on the patio, awaiting further developments. "It's tough being a cop and a new dad. You don't get any sleep, since the kid keeps you up all night. And you still have to deal with the scum of the earth on a daily basis, working a job that puts a lot of stress on a person. I'd say it's a miracle he didn't overdose sooner. And maybe now he'll get the help he needs to kick the habit. He can join one of those rehab clinics."

"I don't think Chase is a drug addict," said Dooley. "Do you, Max?"

"No, I don't think so either," I said.

"I wouldn't be too sure about that, you guys," said Harriet. "Brutus is right. Chase has been under a lot of pressure lately. And let's not forget that it's probably easy for him to get his hands on the stuff. When a drug dealer is arrested, what happens to his stash? It's put in the police precinct evidence locker. And who has access to this locker? The police. So the stuff is simply sitting there, waiting to be taken."

"The temptation finally became too much for him," Brutus said, nodding. "So he took it. Put his hand in the cookie jar. And so he became addicted. The man is only human, after all."

"He should have known better, though," said Harriet. "As a new dad, with a family at home, he should have said no—no way am I going to succumb to the temptation."

"I won't conceal the fact that I'm disappointed," Brutus agreed. "I expected more from him."

"Okay, but if he didn't take the stuff himself," I said, trying to lead the conversation in a different, more productive direction, "that means someone else gave it to him. On purpose, presumably. Which means someone tried to poison Chase. Possibly even kill him."

Now I had the attention of my friends. "Kill Chase?" asked Dooley. "Oh, Max, but that's awful!"

"I know. But it's something we have to consider. If he's being targeted, these people will have found out by now that their attempt on his life has failed. Which means they might try again."

"But we have to tell Odelia! She has to protect him!"

"I'm sure Odelia is thinking the exact same thing I'm thinking," I told my friend. "Which is probably the reason she's staying with Chase tonight at the hospital. To make sure nothing happens to him."

At least I hoped this was the case. But knowing Odelia, she wouldn't believe for one second that her husband was an addict. She would realize what was going on, and keep an eye on him.

"So what we have to figure out is who is behind this attempt on Chase's life. And why," I said.

But Brutus and Harriet were both shaking their heads. "Max, you're delusional," said Brutus. "Clearly Chase is an addict. He fits all the criteria. There was no attempt on his life. You're making all this up simply because you refuse to see the facts."

Which was exactly the same thing I could have told him. But since I didn't want to get into a big argument, I kept my tongue. Instead I gave myself up to thought: when could Chase have been poisoned? And by whom? And most importantly: why?

It certainly was food for thought, and unfortunately I didn't have a lot to go on. The fact that Odelia was at the hospital and thus unavailable to carry out the investigation didn't help.

But at some point Chase would be discharged, and he would be eager to investigate his own poisoning. Which meant we simply had to be patient for now, and trust that Odelia realized what we were up against.

A strong odor of bleach permeated the air, coming at us from every side. The moment she arrived home, Marge had started assisting her mom in her endeavor to clean the entire house. And next door Francine was going through the same ritual.

"I like bleach," Dooley announced as we all took a sniff at the air, redolent now with the chlorine scent of the powerful disinfectant. "In fact I love it. I can smell it all day long."

I have to admit I also enjoy the smell of the stuff. It has something very appealing. Brutus and Harriet didn't seem to agree, for they both wrinkled up their noses in a display of disgust. "Yuck," said Brutus, making his opinion perfectly clear to any observer. "It stinks."

"I prefer roses," Harriet chimed in. "Or lavender."

"Some of these cleaning products contain both," Dooley knew.

Obviously Marge and Gran weren't taking half measures. By the smell of things they were using gallons of the stuff. Pretty soon the whole house would have been disinfected, which was fine by me.

Night had fallen, and Harriet and Brutus announced their desire to leave for cat choir.

"You can't go to cat choir," I said. "You'll only infect others, and we can't do that."

"Not go to cat choir!" Harriet gasped in shock. "Max, are you crazy!"

"We have to go, Maxie baby," said Brutus. "We never miss cat choir. It's our sacred duty to attend."

"And besides, I want a word with Shanille. I'm convinced she's the one who gave me these cooties."

"I thought you said it was Clarice?" I asked.

"And now I think it was Shanille. She rubbed against me last week. And didn't Vena say it's physical contact that transmits these awful little beasts?"

"It's not a beast, it's a fungus," I said.

"Whatever," she said with a wave of her paw. "I know Shanille gave me this thing, and I want her to apologize to me." She raised her chin defiantly. "So I'm going to cat choir, Max, whether you like it or not."

"I'm also going," said Brutus. "I want a word with Kingman."

"You think Kingman gave you ringworm?" I asked.

"Well..." He looked nervous all of a sudden.

"Just spit it out, snuggle bear," said Harriet.

"I may have given *him* the disease," said Brutus. "You see, last night, long before we were aware we had this thing, I gave Kingman a hug. So now I want to tell him maybe he should pay a visit to Vena."

"Oh, dear," I said. Kingman is pretty much the unofficial feline mayor of Hampton Cove. And if he had ringworm, that meant that the entire cat population of our town had it, since Kingman is a very sociable creature. Which meant we would all have to go into some form of quarantine, and the sale of bleach would probably shoot through the roof in the next few weeks. "Maybe you should go," I said therefore. "To warn the others that they might all have ringworm. And that their humans should take them to see Vena."

"And how are they going to transmit that particular message, Max?" asked Harriet sweetly. "None of them can talk to their humans, remember?"

"Okay, so maybe we better tell Odelia to write an article informing local pet parents that ringworm is doing the rounds," I said. "Or maybe Charlene could publish a PSA advising them of same."

"Vena will have a lot of business," said Brutus with a grin.

"I do wonder where this all started," said Harriet.

It reminded me of an episode where we all got infected with fleas. It took us a while to find out who the patient zero had been, but we finally did. I didn't think we'd have the same luck now. It's probably a lot harder to figure out who starts a fungus. And besides, the main thing was to get rid of the stuff, not to investigate its source.

"For all we know we could have gotten it from a human," said Brutus. "This stuff spreads from species to species, doesn't it?"

"It does," I confirmed. "It affects humans, cats, dogs..."

"Dogs!" Harriet cried. Her eyes had immediately turned to the hedge that divides our backyard from the next. "I was chatting with Rufus last week," she said, referring to the Trappers' sheepdog. "And I have to say at some point he was standing very close to me. Very close indeed!"

"There really is no point, Harriet," I said. "We could have gotten it from anyone. And they could all have gotten it from us. We're in this together now, so there's no use pointing the blame."

"I guess," she said, but her eyes were flashing as she stared in the direction of the Trapper backyard, where Rufus lives. Clearly she needed someone to blame, whether it was Clarice or Shanille or Rufus.

"Let's tell Marge to talk to Marcie," I said. "So she can have Rufus examined. And she should do the same thing with Kurt and Fifi." Fifi being Kurt Mayfield's Yorkie and a very dear friend of ours.

"A bleach bomb is coming, you guys," Dooley said with an ecstatic smile. "It's going to be the best time ever!"

CHAPTER 27

It took Francine a lot longer to clean Odelia's place than she had anticipated. The house might not be all that big, but it still offered a lot of surfaces that needed to be cleaned. And when you considered all of the cupboards and wardrobes and the miles and miles of shelves, it was going to be a much bigger job than she was prepared to handle. So after having done a deep cleaning of the room she was currently staying in, in other words the main bedroom, she decided to leave the rest of the house for another day. One room she definitely was not going to touch was the guest bedroom, with its freaky big-ass spider. Yuck!

And she was enjoying a nice cup of coffee—the tasty caramel variety—when her eye caught movement in the backyard. A molehill had just popped up where no molehill had been only moments before.

"That darn..." she grumbled, remembering the oath she had sworn that she was going to take care of that mole one way or another.

So she took out her phone and googled 'How to get rid of moles.' Castor oil seemed the way to go, and as luck would have it, she had seen a plastic jug of castor oil in the cabinet under the kitchen sink. She took it out, along with a bucket, and started adding the oil to the bucket before filling it up with water.

"That should do the trick," she grunted with satisfaction. She took the bucket outside, and started pouring its contents on top of the molehill. The mixture quickly seeped into the ground, and presumably did whatever it was supposed to do down there, namely sending a clear message to the mole that it was no longer welcome there.

Odelia would be happy, she thought with satisfaction. She felt a little guilty for staying in the woman's house, driving away her cats, and generally making a nuisance of herself, especially now that her husband was in the hospital. Odelia's mom had told her that the cop would be fine, but that he would have to stay at the hospital for another night, and maybe even longer. In spite of her misgivings about life in boring suburbia her heart bled for the couple, and getting rid of these moles was the least she could do.

A nice surprise when they finally got home again.

And it was with uplifted mood that she returned the bucket and bottle of castor oil to their designated place underneath the sink. A good job well done!

* * *

Jackie sniffed the air in the tunnel she had just dug and thought she smelled something extremely disagreeable. She sniffed some more and then she knew it: castor oil! Gah! She hated castor oil. In fact all moles did. It wasn't so much the smell as the composition of the substance that made her stomach turn.

Now how in God's name had the stuff ended up in her

precious tunnel? And it was a great tunnel, having yielded a lot of prime grub.

She quickly returned to her burrow to report to her husband.

Dave was enjoying a nice rest, lying on his back and generally dreaming of good things to come, when his slumber was rudely interrupted by the arrival of his spouse.

"They're pouring castor oil into our tunnels, Dave," she lamented. "Can you believe it?"

"So?" he said. "Go talk to that cat friend of yours. If what you were telling me is true he'll be able to talk to his human, and tell her to cut it out."

"I know, but there's a new sheriff in town. Her name is Francine, and she reminds me of the idiot who set off firecrackers in our home that time—remember him?"

"Do I?" said Dave with a frown. "That fool almost killed us! Are you telling me he's here?"

"No, she just reminds me of him. Not sure why, but at least she's not using firecrackers. Instead she's pouring castor oil in my new tunnel."

"Nasty woman," Dave growled. "Looks like we'll have to move again, huh?"

"Looks like it," Jackie confirmed. "Unless..."

"Unless what?"

"Unless I can convince Max to work his magic."

"Max being..."

"The tubby orange cat I was telling you about."

"Right, right."

"I'll go and talk to him now. This castor oil business has got to stop. It's not nice."

"Oh, and tell Max to tell his human to water the lawn. Place is parched!"

Dave was right as always, Jackie thought as she started her trek to the surface. She passed the kitchen, where a couple of juicy worms were waiting to be devoured, then passed the nursery, where her four babies were napping, the sight of which never failed to put a smile on her face. Finally she reached the surface, and cautiously stuck her head out. She glanced left and right but when she couldn't detect any sign of the woman or her castor oil, she ventured out into the garden, in search of Max and Dooley.

CHAPTER 28

Mike wasn't used to being home alone. With Yvonne out of town, and Emily, the house felt eerily empty and cold. The servants had all gone home, and now he was all alone in that big place that his great-grandfather had built. Seated behind his desk in his office, he wondered not for the first time why neither his granddad or his father had ever mentioned that diary. Apparently it had been lost in the mists of time.

His phone, which was lying on the desk, started vibrating and he picked it up. "Yes, Dad?"

"Are you sure you don't want me to join you for that meeting tomorrow morning, son?"

"That's all right, Dad. I think I can handle it."

"Is she bringing the diary?"

"She is bringing the diary."

"Finally. And you have arranged for the specialist to take a closer look at the thing?"

"I have. James Van Der Beek is the pre-eminent specialist on antiquities and old documents. He'll be able to tell us if the thing is real or not."

"Well, let's hope for our sake it is. Real, I mean. Would be a pity if it turns out to be a fake after all."

"I doubt that very much. It has to be real. And it stands to reason that there would be lithium in the old mine." It was true what Francine had told him: potash and lithium were often found in the same deposits. Which begged a very important question. "Why didn't you or grandpa ever look for lithium, Dad?"

"Because we never thought it was there! All the experts convinced us the mine was exhausted, and that keeping it running was economically unsound. So we closed it up and that was that. Or at least that's what we thought. Until Francine popped up with that diary of hers."

It was a miracle. Just when they needed the money, a cousin he didn't know existed showed up with a diary he hadn't known existed either. It was the answer to all of his prayers. Almost too good to be true!

"Well, good thing she did," he told his father. "Without that lithium we wouldn't stand a chance."

"I know," said his dad with a sigh.

Of course he had immediately checked Francine's antecedents. But as far as he could make out they were genuine enough. Ebenezer Knight hadn't exactly been known for his fidelity, and the fact that he had started a second family in a different state wasn't as surprising as it should have been. Francine had provided him with the necessary birth certificates and it was right there in black and white: Ebenezer Knight, using the name Jack Cooper, had fathered a daughter named Helen, Francine's grandmother, making her the distant cousin he had never met, and whose existence had been a secret all this time.

She hadn't even known herself, until her grandmother had died, and on her deathbed had told her the truth about her ancestry. She had also left her the diary, containing the bombshell revelation about the lithium. It was exactly what Mike needed. Tomorrow he'd have the diary checked for its authenticity, and if everything panned out, which he hoped and expected it would, they could proceed from there.

"Why don't I join you anyway?" asked his dad. "Just to be on the safe side. And besides, I wouldn't mind finally meeting this mysterious cousin of yours. Does she look like a Knight?"

"She does, actually," he confirmed. "She reminds me of Grandma. At least the pictures I've seen of her."

"Stands to reason," said his dad. "Considering your grandmother and Francine's grandmother were half-sisters, even if they weren't aware of each other's existence. It's a crazy story, my boy."

"It is," he said. "But it's exactly what we need right now."

"You can say that again. Have you told Yvonne?"

"Not yet. No sense in getting her hopes up before I've got this thing in the bag."

"Absolutely. Let me know how it goes?"

"Of course, Dad."

After he had disconnected he let his mind briefly dwell on some of the projects that he had failed at these last couple of years. It had put a considerable strain on his marriage. Financial difficulties had a way of doing that. Which is why he hadn't told Yvonne about Francine. He fervently hoped this was the one. If it wasn't, he had a feeling he wouldn't only kiss his home and his business goodbye, but also his marriage, and possibly even any visitation rights to Emily.

He closed his eyes with a pained expression on his face. That was the last thing he needed right now. Another marriage crisis and possibly even a divorce and a drawn-out custody rights battle.

Suddenly tomorrow couldn't come fast enough.

CHAPTER 29

Lucky for us it was a balmy evening, so Dooley and I slept on the porch swing. At least we were still welcome there, and Marge had even put down pillows to make us more comfortable. As long as we were suffering from this ringworm, I guess this is what our lives would be like: shunned from our own homes, and prohibited to make personal contact with our own humans.

We had told Marge and Gran about our assessment that probably a lot more cats would have contracted the infection, and maybe dogs, too. They had shared a look of horror, and had immediately got in touch with Charlene, the town mayor and Uncle Alec's girlfriend, to distribute a PSA. People had to check their pets for signs of the infection, and if in doubt they would have to get in touch with the vet. I could already predict a lot of wailing and gnashing of teeth amongst the pet population in our small town.

"Maybe Harriet is right, and we should have joined cat choir," said Dooley. "After all, if everybody has this ringbeard—"

"Ringworm."

"—then it doesn't matter if we visit with our friends or not."

He had a point, of course. Apparently this disease or infection was very democratic, in that it liked to infect everyone in equal measure.

"We can't go, Dooley," I said nevertheless. "We have to keep an eye on Francine, remember? She's getting a visit from an associate tonight? And I don't know about you, but I for one am very curious to find out what this visit is all about."

"Probably an old boyfriend," said Dooley. "She misses him and so she's asked him to pay her a visit, even though she's not supposed to, since she's officially undercover."

"Not exactly undercover," I said with a smile. "She's in hiding from some bad people that are after her." It was all connected to the old Knight mine, apparently, even though I had a hard time figuring out how the pieces of the puzzle fit, exactly. Which is why I wanted to listen in on that meeting, and hopefully find out more.

And I'd just opened my mouth to suggest a possible approach, when a small, brown furry creature appeared on the porch, clearly eager to have speech with us. She looked extremely distraught.

"Jackie!" I said. "What's wrong?"

"Oh, there you are," said Jackie. "I've been looking for you guys. This Francine person has gone and poured a bucket of castor oil into my best tunnel," she lamented. "And from what I've seen of this woman she won't hesitate to pour a couple of buckets more. So isn't there anything you can do, Max? Maybe talk to that human of yours and tell her to stop making our lives miserable? I mean, Dave and I are simply going about our business, trying to be the best neighbors we can be, and here this psychopath goes and pours castor oil on top of our heads! I ask you: is this nice? Is this neighborly? No, it is not!"

"I'll talk to Odelia," I said. "But unfortunately she's at the hospital right now."

"Chase has become a drug addict," Dooley said. "Or at least that seems to be the general opinion."

"It's not the general opinion," I countered. "It's Brutus and Harriet's opinion. Marge doesn't believe that Chase is a drug addict, and neither does Tex."

"Well, be that as it may," said Jackie. "If you could talk to Odelia when she gets back? Castor oil is the last thing I need right now. With four mouths to feed and all the work we put into digging those tunnels and creating our new lair it's a little hard to have to up sticks and move next door on a moment's notice."

"I wouldn't move next door if I were you," I said. "Kurt Mayfield may have become a lot mellower since he found love, but I'm sure he wouldn't take kindly to you and Dave moving into his backyard."

"Castor oil would be the least of your worries," Dooley added.

"Oh, we were once bombed in our beds," said Jackie. "So we're used to this type of behavior. But we hadn't settled down back then, and we have now. And it's a lot harder to move house when you've got four little ones depending on you for their daily grub of grubs."

"That's right. You guys eat a lot of grubs, don't you?" I said.

"Grubs, earthworms, centipedes, beetles… You name it, we eat it," said Jackie proudly.

"Is it true that moles can eat their body weight in food?" asked Dooley. "And that you can dig fifteen feet per hour?" Clearly he'd been surfing the Discovery Channel website.

"All true," said Jackie. "We're master diggers, buddy. And

now if you'll excuse me, I've got tunnels to dig and worms to catch. You won't forget to talk to one of your humans on our behalf, will you?"

"We won't forget," I promised.

"I hate castor oil," she said, and took off.

Marge had stepped out of the house and joined us for a moment. She was clutching a cup of hot tea in both hands and took a seat at the edge of the swing. "Who was that you were talking to just now?"

"Oh, that was Jackie," I said.

"She's a mole," Dooley explained. "Only Francine has been pouring castor oil down her tunnels, and now she wants us to talk to you and ask you to tell Francine to cut it out."

"Francine is pouring castor oil down the molehills in Odelia's backyard?" Marge sounded very much surprised. "She shouldn't do that. It's not her place."

"So maybe you could talk to her?" I suggested. "Jackie is very upset, and so is her husband Dave and their four little ones."

Marge smiled. "You guys lead interesting lives, don't you?"

"Harriet thinks that Chase is a drug addict, Marge," said Dooley, broaching a topic that was clearly very important to him. "Is it true? Is he an addict?"

Marge's smile vanished as if wiped away with a squeegee. "I doubt it," she said immediately. "Chase is simply not the type. It's more likely that he ingested the stuff by accident. But how it happened, exactly, and when, is something for my brother to figure out. As soon as Chase is awake, Alec will talk to him, and hopefully together they will get to the truth."

"He probably ingested it at the office, right?" I said. "Maybe someone put it in his coffee?"

Marge stared down at her cup of tea for a moment. "It's possible," she allowed. "But like I said, at this point we have no idea how it happened. Which makes it all the more scary since we don't know if it was done deliberately or by accident."

"If he was deliberately drugged, we're talking murder," I said.

"Attempted murder, yes," said Marge. "Which is something Alec is seriously considering. But let's not get ahead of ourselves. For all we know it was an accident, and Chase simply happened to drink from a cup that wasn't his and got the stuff into his system that way."

"Which means there's a drug addict at the police precinct," said Dooley, displaying an iron sense of logic.

Marge patted him on the head. "Let's just wait and see, shall we? Alec knows what he's doing. He'll figure it out."

She returned indoors, then changed her mind and crossed the short distance to her daughter's backyard, in search of Francine. No more moles would be obstructed in carrying out their lawful duty.

CHAPTER 30

It was at some point during the night that Chase finally opened his eyes. He looked around and when his gaze fell on Odelia, he frowned. "Where am I? What's going on?" he asked in a croaky voice.

"Oh, babe!" she said, and threw herself on top of him before realizing she probably shouldn't and immediately retreating again.

"Am I in a hospital?" he asked, looking around.

"You are, you are, but now you're fine." She was so happy that tears were trickling down her cheeks as she clutched his hands in hers. "You fell into a coma, so we took you to the hospital."

He grimaced. "I knew it. I should never have eaten that last prawn. I thought it smelled funny."

"It wasn't the prawn," said Odelia. "You were drugged, babe."

"Drugged? What do you mean?"

"Someone drugged you with GHB."

"The date rape drug?"

She nodded. "In combination with the sedative Dad gave

you it put you in a coma. The doctors told us you'll be fine, but it was touch and go for a while." She swiped at her teary cheeks. "I thought I lost you."

He smiled a weak smile, and it was a sight for sore eyes. "You can't lose me. I'm like a bad penny. I keep turning up when you least expect it." He turned serious again. "So who drugged me, do they know?"

She shook her head. "Uncle Alec will want to talk to you. They want to figure out what happened."

He grabbed at his head. "How long have I been here?"

"Yesterday afternoon. It's actually the cats that raised the alarm when you wouldn't wake up."

"Thank God for the cats," he muttered as he squeezed his eyes tightly shut. "My head is killing me."

"I'll call for the nurse," said Odelia. "Tell them you're awake."

"Wait. GHB is a fast-acting drug. Doesn't take more than fifteen or twenty minutes to have an effect. So I must have taken it shortly before I went to sleep." He frowned as he tried to think back. "My bottle," he said finally. "The water bottle I always take to the gym. Tell Alec to look for it and have it tested."

"Where did you leave it?"

"One of the cupboards in the kitchen."

"Oh, no."

"What?"

"Francine. If she gets thirsty, she might grab your bottle."

She took out her phone, but when she tried to call Francine, the call went straight to voicemail. Which was understandable since it was the middle of the night. So she left an urgent message that their house guest shouldn't drink from any water bottles she found in the kitchen.

They didn't need a second person going into a coma.

* * *

WE'D BEEN HIDING under those rose bushes for what felt like half the night, waiting for Francine to meet her mystery man. The important thing was that we shouldn't be seen, since Odelia's guest seemed to harbor an aversion to cats that bordered on the irrational.

"What if she snuck out of the house through the front door and met this man in a different location?" asked Dooley.

"She wouldn't do that. She's not supposed to be seen," I said. "She's hiding from the people who are trying to find her, remember?" So it stood to reason that when she did meet this man, it would be right there, in the backyard. Or the house. In which case we should be able to see the man and sneak closer so we could spy on the meeting.

An owl was hooting in a nearby tree, and I imagined that Jackie and Dave were busy digging tunnels and catching dinner—or possibly breakfast—for their young. Harriet and Brutus still hadn't returned, and I was starting to question the wisdom of skipping cat choir simply so we could spend all night underneath the rose bushes.

But finally our patience was rewarded when a creaking sound nearby told us something was happening. As we looked up, we saw that a man had climbed over the fence and was entering the backyard, stealthily making his way to the house. As if she had sensed his presence, the kitchen door opened and Francine appeared. She quickly walked to the back of the garden and whispered, "Not here. Let's meet in the field." She was pointing in the direction of the field that lies behind the backyard.

"I just climbed that fence!" the man lamented.

"And now you're going to climb it again."

"And so are we," I told Dooley.

"Goodie! It's finally happening, Max!"

We watched as first the man and then Francine scaled that fence. For her convenience Francine had had the foresight to place a ladder against it, which made it a lot easier to climb over.

"Looks like she made her preparations," I told Dooley as we put our paws on the first step, then made our way up and over.

"Did you get a good look at the man?" he asked.

"Enough to see that he doesn't have a beard," I returned.

"That means it must be him!"

"Hey, where are you going?" asked a little voice behind us. It was Jackie, and she was staring up at us with unbridled curiosity.

"We're spying on Francine," I told her.

"She's conducting a secret meeting!" Dooley added.

"Oh, how exciting! Can I join you guys? The kids are asleep, and so is Dave, and I've dug all my tunnels for the day so I've got nothing to do."

"Be my guest," I said, and watched as the tiny mole, instead of climbing the ladder, started digging a tunnel underneath the fence.

"I wish I could do that," said Dooley. "Look at her go, Max!"

"She is fast," I admitted.

By the time we were over that fence, Jackie had already resurfaced, and now joined us as we made our way across the field, in the direction of the sounds of Francine meeting her mystery man.

It didn't take us long to locate them, and then we hunkered down and listened in.

"Okay, so you know what to do for the big meeting with Mike tomorrow?" Francine was asking.

"Of course I know what to do. What do you think I am? Stupid?"

"You have been known to make mistakes, Brian."

"Oh, and you haven't? Remember that time you were going to marry Little Lord Fauntleroy and you called him by the wrong name?"

"That was an honest mistake," she said. "The important thing is that you won't be late."

"I won't," he promised. "So how are you holding up?" He was gesturing with his head to the house.

"I've got the place to myself. Like I told you over the phone, the cop is in a coma and he's at the hospital right now with his wife."

"And the cats?"

"Don't start about those cats again, Brian."

"I'm telling you, there's something funny about those cats!"

"Cats can't talk to people, dummy. That only happens in Disney movies." When he continued to stare at her, she sighed. "Okay, I got rid of them, just as you said. But it wasn't easy. These people are cat crazy."

"See? I told you. The whole family is the same way."

"They can't talk to cats. That's simply impossible."

"I don't know how they do it. All I know is what I've been told. The family has a reputation in this town. Everyone I talked to said so. Especially the grandmother, the mother and the daughter. And the consensus seems to be that those cats can't be trusted. They spy on people and get them into all kinds of trouble when they're not careful. They spy and your friend Odelia writes it all down in that paper of hers."

"Anyway," she said, tiring of the topic. "I've already got your next job lined up."

"You have? Nice big one?"

"It's connected to this one. Something I discovered in the course of my prep work. How much do you know about horses?"

He groaned. "First cats, now horses? What's next: flying pigs?"

"Pigs don't fly, you idiot. Just like cats don't talk."

"Wait! Did you see that?"

We all watched where Brian was looking. The night sky was lighting up with the blue flashing light of a police vehicle. Though it could have been an ambulance, of course, or even a fire engine.

"It's the cops!" said Brian.

"Or it could be the ambulance returning with Odelia and her husband." She gave her associate a look of suspicion. "You didn't by any chance have anything to do with putting him into that coma, did you?"

Brian gave her a triumphant grin. "And what if I did?"

"Brian! I told you to be discreet!"

"I was discreet. I found out what gym he goes to, and I pulled a quick switcheroo on his water bottle. He never saw me, I swear! A couple of drops of GHB and presto. Annoying cop out of commission."

"You almost killed him, you idiot!"

Brian looked perplexed. "Impossible. I didn't give him that much."

"He took a sleeping pill on top of the GHB you fed him, which put him into that coma."

"Now why would he go and do a stupid thing like that?"

"I better get back," said Francine when the flashing blue lights were coming closer. "Looks like they're heading this way. They'll think it's suspicious when I'm not there when they arrive."

"You could tell them you've gone for a walk."

"After I told them I was afraid for my life?"

"About that. I may have a lead on the feller who was chasing you."

"Who?"

"Kevin Robinson. Nasty piece of work. Works in close collaboration with Steve Campbell. Both of them are known enforcers for the mob."

She moved her face closer to his and stabbed a finger in his chest. "Just keep them off my back. I don't need this right now."

"Sure, sure," said Brian appeasingly.

Francine left the meeting, and quickly returned to the house. Brian stood staring after her for a moment, rubbing his chin. Then he shook his head and left in the other direction, crossing the field and presumably heading for his car parked on the next street.

"You guys!" said Jackie suddenly. "I think I know that guy!"

"You know this Brian fellow?" I asked.

"It's the same guy who tried to blow Dave and me up with his firecrackers. The one I told you about? Only he had a beard last time I saw him. A ratty specimen that made him look like a tramp."

"I thought you said Francine reminded you of him?"

"She does." She smiled triumphantly. "She was there. I remember now. I saw the two of them together one time. They must be an item."

"They do seem to know each other pretty well," I said.

"It's uncanny how well you can see," said Dooley, who had been staring at our new friend with admiration written all over his features. "And here I always thought moles were practically blind."

"We're not blind, exactly," said Jackie, simpering modestly. "But I have to admit my eyesight is exceptionally excellent for a mole."

"I'll say," I said. "What else do you remember about Brian?"

"Only that he hates moles. And that his house was always a mess and so were his clothes."

It was true that Brian's personal apparel left something to be desired. Then again, when you conduct secret midnight meetings dress code is probably the last thing on your mind.

"Okay, we better run," I said. "We don't want to miss Chase's triumphant return from the hospital."

CHAPTER 31

Unfortunately it wasn't Chase who had arrived, or Odelia, but Uncle Alec. When nobody answered the door—understandable at such a late hour—he had snuck around the back and tried to enter the house through the kitchen, succeeding because Francine had left the door unlocked. Unwise, I would have said, considering the attempted break-in we had that afternoon.

We snuck up to the house, and in through the pet flap, and arrived just in time to witness the scene where Uncle Alec met Francine for the first time. She must have surprised him in the kitchen, for he looked a little startled.

"Looking for something?" she asked, an edge to her voice. Clearly she thought he was a burglar of some kind.

"Oh, hi," he said. "I'm Odelia's uncle, and you must be Francine Martin?"

"That's right. How did you get in?"

"Well, the door was open," he said, gesturing to the kitchen door. He caught sight of me, Dooley and Jackie and frowned. But then pretended not to see us. A wise move, considering Francine's hang-up about cats. "Look, I can see how this looks," said Uncle Alec, holding up his hands. "Especially considering the fact that a burglar tried to break in next door this afternoon. But I really am Odelia's uncle. I can show you my badge, if you like?"

"Please do," said Francine curtly. Once Uncle Alec had produced his badge, her demeanor went through a remarkable change. She relaxed visibly. "I really thought you were a burglar," she told him. "So what can I do for you, Chief?"

"Odelia sent me," said Uncle Alec. "Chase regained consciousness, and he told her he thinks his water bottle was spiked. Must have happened at the gym. So naturally she was worried that you would find his bottle and drink from it and get the same poison into your system. Also, that bottle is evidence now."

"I didn't see a bottle," she said. "And I certainly didn't drink from it. But it's good to know that Odelia is looking out for me. So how is Chase? Will he be all right?"

"She's a great actress, Max," Dooley whispered. "She knows perfectly well what happened to Chase but she's hiding it!"

"I know," I whispered back.

"So who's the big fella?" asked Jackie.

"Odelia's uncle," I said. "He's the chief of police."

"Oh, good. Let's hope he arrests her."

"For what? She didn't do anything wrong that we know."

"She's lying about that water bottle!" Dooley said.

"I don't think Uncle Alec can arrest her for lying, Dooley."

"Well, he should. Obviously she's a very bad person and she's up to a lot of no good!"

Unfortunately our conversation had attracted Francine's attention, and she now glanced down to where we had been hiding. "Those cats again!" she growled. "Shoo! Get out! Get out now!"

"Those are Odelia's cats," Uncle Alec pointed out. "Don't

you like cats?" He was frowning, and rightly so. Hating cats might not constitute a crime, but in my book it's certainly a misdemeanor.

Francine backtracked. "No, it's just that... I'm allergic."

"Liar!" Dooley said. "Brian told her Odelia can talk to her cats, so she made sure she got rid of us!"

"Okay, so can you help me find that bottle, Francine?" asked Uncle Alec. "It's important that we find it and have it examined at the lab."

"Absolutely," said Francine, and started opening cupboards left and right, in search of Chase's water bottle. Meanwhile Uncle Alec searched the living room for any trace of that now infamous bottle. And that's when I saw that Francine suddenly put her hands on a clear plastic bottle that was right next to the big tub of protein powder Chase likes to use. She glanced at Uncle Alec, who was looking underneath the coffee table, then quickly stuffed the bottle inside the trash bin and arranged some garbage on top of it.

"She's hiding the bottle!" Dooley cried. "Max, did you see that?!"

"I saw," I said. "And she won't get away with this, Dooley."

"Uncle Alec!" Dooley cried. "The bottle is in the trash!"

Uncle Alec looked up. "Did you find it?" he asked Francine.

She shook her head. "Unfortunately not, Chief. Maybe he took it upstairs when he went to bed?"

"I'll look in the bedroom," Odelia's uncle grunted, and stomped up the stairs.

The moment he was gone, Francine took the bottle out of the trash, poured its contents down the sink, wiped the bottle clean with a dishrag, then crushed it with her hands and stuffed it into the trash bin again. She took out the bin liner, stood still for a moment, listening intently, then hurried out the door, trash bag in hand, presumably to put out the trash and remove all evidence of her partner Brian's wrongdoing.

"Max, did you see!" Dooley cried. "She's destroying the evidence!"

"I know," I said. "And we'll tell Odelia as soon as we see her. But right now there isn't a whole lot we can do, unfortunately."

"I told you these people were bad news," said Jackie. "Anyone who pours castor oil down my front door and puts firecrackers in my tunnels is bad news in my book."

"Cat hating, mole harassing, evidence destroying," Dooley summed up. "The list of crimes keeps getting longer and longer."

"Uh-oh," I said. Francine had turned her attention to us, and from the way she was looking I had a feeling our presence was no longer required or desired.

"Didn't I tell you to get out?!" she hissed, and took off her shoe. Before she could throw it, we decided to beat a hasty retreat. And so moments later we were hurrying out through the pet flap in single file: two cats and one mole. Clearly Francine's problem with cats extended beyond suspecting us of being spies!

"Oh, boy," said Dooley. "Have we got a story to tell Odelia!"

Upstairs, the light was on in the main bedroom. We could have told Uncle Alec he was wasting his time. But unfortunately we couldn't. We could have woken up Gran or Marge, but there hardly seemed any point. We knew the culprit, and we knew what Francine had done. She wouldn't get away with this.

I wondered what she was up to, though. She had mentioned something about horses. And about a meeting with Mike tomorrow. That would be Mike Knight, and the meeting was probably connected to that lithium mine. So what was she planning? And what did she need Brian for? It certainly didn't bode well, that much was obvious. And what part did Odelia play in all of this? Why had Francine selected our home, of all homes, to hide from this Kevin Robinson? It was all very mysterious, and frankly I was afraid for Odelia. If these people had managed to put Chase in the hospital, what else were they capable of?

CHAPTER 32

Look, I'm fully aware of the old cliché image of the cats digging through the trash, all right? But you have to admit that Dooley and I had a good reason to do exactly that. In our defense, some very important evidence had been dumped in the trash that we needed to fish out before it was taken to some landfill.

And so no less than ten minutes after Francine had put out the trash, Dooley and I, with the valued assistance of Jackie, were ripping open that bag and checking its contents. And I don't use the term 'valued' idly, since it soon became obvious why moles are considered premier diggers. The speed and skill Jackie used to go through the contents of that bag were stunning, and left me feeling entirely inadequate as a trash digger.

"Pretty amazing, eh, Max?" said Dooley as we stood back and watched her work her magic.

"I've never seen anything like it," I agreed.

"Now I understand why moles can create such an elaborate maze of tunnels. They're so fast!"

"They are fast. And efficient!"

It didn't take her more than a minute to find that bottle and alert us of its presence. And we would have taken possession of the valuable item if not suddenly a shoe would have whizzed past my ear. As it was, the thrower of the projectile turned out to be Kurt Mayfield, of all people, apparently out late for a walk. Alongside him was Fifi, who gave us a look of embarrassment at the behavior of her human.

"I'm sorry," she said. "I guess Kurt still isn't very fond of you guys."

"Shoo," said Kurt. "Go on—shoo! Digging through the trash like that. Bunch of street cats..." Then he took a closer look and must have recognized Dooley and me. "By golly, if it ain't Odelia's cats! What are you doing out here? Looking for food, I'll bet." He turned to Fifi. "Poor creatures must be starving."

"Their human is in the hospital," Fifi reminded him. "So they must be hungry and homeless right now. And desperate."

"We're neither hungry nor homeless," I said, eager to remove this stain on our character. "For your information we're on a mission to retrieve some very important and incriminating evidence from this here bag of trash. And with the help of our friend Jackie we managed to find it and are now in the process of securing it for police inspection."

"Poor creatures," Kurt repeated as he picked up his shoe and put it back on. "You must be starving. Did they lock you out of your home? Is that what happened?" He thought for a moment, then made a decision. "Let's go," he said. And when we didn't make to follow him, he said with more emphasis. "Let's go, I said! Now!"

"Are you sure he didn't serve in the military, Fifi?" asked Dooley.

"Pretty sure," said Fifi. "Just do as he says. He gets cranky when you don't."

And so we followed our neighbor as he led the way to his own home.

"Does his invitation extend to me as well, you think?" asked Jackie.

"I very much doubt that," I said. "So please guard that bottle with your life, Jackie. Don't let anyone touch it, you hear?"

She gave me a puzzled look. "Tough to guard a bottle, Max. I'm just a tiny mole, after all."

"Use your imagination!" I said, but then was spurred on by Kurt to follow him into his home.

He opened the door for us, and led us into the kitchen, where he pointed to a very large bowl filled with kibble. "Dig in," he said curtly. And when Fifi gave a cry of dismay, he added, "Oh, don't be like that, Fifi. There's plenty more where that came from. Never heard about sharing is caring? Dig in, I tell you!" he roared when Dooley and I stood around for a moment, waiting until Fifi gave her approval. We were in her home, after all.

"It's all right," she said finally. "Like Kurt says: sharing is caring. And you guys are my friends, after all."

"Why, thanks, Fifi," said Dooley, and gratefully started gobbling up some of that dog kibble. "Pretty decent stuff," he told me. "Not as tasty as our own eats but not bad."

And since Kurt was staring at me with arms crossed in front of his chest, I joined my friend and started imbibing some of Fifi's food. Dooley was right. It wasn't bad at all. Clearly Kurt had splurged and only bought his precious pet the good stuff. None of that store brand grub but definitely premium brand.

"And if you need a place to stay for the night," Kurt added after he had grunted with satisfaction, "you can always crash on the couch. I'm sure Fifi won't mind. Isn't that right, Fifi?" he added with a touch of menace in his voice.

Fifi nodded quickly. "I don't mind at all," she said, even though I could tell that she preferred to have the house to herself. And who could blame her? Today it was Dooley and me. Tomorrow Kurt might invite all the cats of the neighborhood into his home.

"He has definitely changed a lot," I told Fifi between two bites.

"Yeah, he has turned a corner," she confirmed. "Gone from grinch to Mr. Hospitality. Just shows you what the power of love can do."

Mrs. Goldstein from next door ambled into the kitchen. Though obviously she didn't live next door anymore but had moved in with Kurt. "What are you doing up so late?" she asked. Then she caught sight of us and her lips formed a perfect Oh. "Aren't those Odelia's cats? What are they doing in here?"

"Chase was taken to the hospital," said Kurt. "And Odelia must be there as well. So the cats got locked out with no food and no shelter. I found them on the street just now digging through the trash."

"Oh, the poor creatures!" said Mrs. Goldstein, clasping her hands together. "Make sure they're fed and taken care of, will you? Odelia will thank you."

"As a rule I'm not very fond of cats," said Kurt ruefully. "But I couldn't just leave them out there like that, now could I? Plus they're friends of Fifi's."

"They're friends of Fifi's? How do you know?"

"Oh, she sneaks next door all the time," said Kurt. "And they sneak into my backyard, too. I always catch them chatting it up."

Mrs. Goldstein laughed. "Chatting it up! Imagine that.

Cats and dogs chatting. You've got a vivid imagination, Kurt Mayfield."

Kurt returned her smile. "I know. Must be living next door to a bunch of cat ladies. Their affection for the weird creatures is beginning to rub off on me."

We had eaten our fill, and Dooley said, "That was very delicious, Mr. Mayfield. But can we go now? Max and I were on a very important mission. You see, someone tried to poison our human, and we caught her destroying evidence, and now we have to save it so she can't get away with it."

"Isn't that cute?" said Mrs. Goldstein, bending to give Dooley a pat on the head. "I used to hate cats, too," she revealed. "But I have to admit these aren't so bad. And my allergy seems to have miraculously cleared up."

"They're all right," Kurt said. "Except when they start their caterwauling. Did I mention that I almost caught a burglar this afternoon? And I could have sworn that these two somehow tried to warn me."

Mrs. Goldstein laughed again. "Oh, Kurt, you're too funny. As if cats are smart enough to do something like that."

"Maybe they are, and maybe they aren't," said Kurt as he gave me a wink. I returned the wink, much to his surprise, and as Dooley and I made our way through the pet flap, I could tell that he was regarding me with a look of bewilderment on his face.

We hurried back to the trash bag and found to our relief that Jackie had brought in reinforcements in the form of her husband Dave and their four kids. They were guarding the evidence with their lives, or at least they put on a good show of doing so. The four little ones were gleefully playing with the garbage, which had now been redistributed all across the sidewalk, while their mommy and daddy looked on with pride written all over their features.

"Oh, Max, this was such a good idea," said Jackie when we

finally caught up with her. "Thanks for the opportunity. The kids are having a ball."

"Hi, Max," said Dave, giving my paw a tap. "Great to meet you."

I took in the mess that had been created and shook my head. "Yeah, great to meet you, too, " I said. "Is there any chance you could, you know, clean this up a little?"

"Clear what up?" asked Dave, not comprehending.

"Well, this. This mess."

"What mess? What are you talking about?"

And so I decided to leave it. It had been a long day filled with excitement and frankly I was too tired to bother. Tomorrow was another day, and hopefully it would be less fraught with anxiety. And just as we were ready to head next door and take a nap on the porch swing, as had been our intention all along, I noticed a car parked across the road with a man behind the wheel who looked very familiar indeed.

It was the very same burglar we had chased away earlier that day!

CHAPTER 33

Just then, Harriet and Brutus returned from a pleasant time at cat choir. They both looked in excellent spirits so obviously a good time was had by all, in spite of the ringworm epidemic raging through the local pet population. When they saw the mess on the sidewalk, they halted. "What happened here?" asked Harriet, who's a stickler for cleanliness and orderliness.

"Nothing," I said. "Don't look now, but the same burglar who tried to burgle the house this afternoon is across the street, sitting in his car and watching the house." Of course Brutus and Harriet immediately looked over. "I said: don't look now!"

"You're right," said Harriet. "It's the same guy. He must have decided to return for an encore." She brightened. "Shall I sing my signature song again, Max? I'm sure he's simply a fan."

"Please don't," I said. "No sense in attracting his attention. Not until he makes his move."

"What move do you think he's going to make?" asked Dooley.

"A dance move," said Brutus acerbically, and laughed at his own joke. When Dooley gave him a look of confusion, he patted him on the back. "Just kidding, buddy."

"Cat choir was obviously a fun affair," I said.

"Oh, it was great," he said. "Turns out all the cats in Hampton Cove have ringworm by now, or at least most of them. So we're all in the same boat. And since no one can infect anyone, we decided not to bother with restrictions and simply have fun."

"What restrictions?" asked Dooley.

"Oh, you know: don't get too close. No physical contact. That sort of thing. But since we're all infected anyway, that doesn't apply."

The little moles were still playing with the refuse, and Harriet eyed them with a look of disapproval. And she probably would have said something if the burglar hadn't decided that the time was right for another attempt at securing for himself some of the spoils of his trade. He carefully closed the door of his car, looked left and right, and crossed the road. For a moment he glanced down at us, but if he recognized us, he didn't give any indication. Clearly he wasn't too worried about an encore from Harriet and her backing vocalists. Instead he disappeared into the front yard, and quickly made his way around the back.

And so we decided to follow and see what he was up to this time. But not before I somehow managed to clasp that water bottle between my teeth and drag it along with me. I deposited it on Marge's porch for safekeeping, and then hurried to join the others—and the burglar.

IT DIDN'T TAKE him long to probe the kitchen door, the sliding glass door, then direct a longing look upstairs.

"You have to hand it to him," I said. "He gets an A for perseverance."

"And stupidity," said Brutus. "Imagine trying to burgle the house of a cop."

"Unless he knows that Chase is in the hospital," I said.

The mole family had followed us into the backyard, and now regarded the burglar with a keen eye. The man had grabbed the drainpipe and was testing it for its capacity to support his weight. Presently he was shimmying his way up the pipe like a professional acrobat. It only took him a few moments to reach the second floor, where he found one of the windows tilted open to let in some of that bracing night air.

I'd never actually seen this, and frankly had believed it impossible, but the burglar made short shrift with the window, tilt position or not, and in mere seconds was already crawling in.

"He's burgling our house!" Dooley cried. "Max, we have to stop him. He'll steal our kibble!"

Harriet cleared her throat. "What do you think, Max? Celine again? Or shall I do Mariah this time?"

But before I could respond, there was some form of commotion upstairs. The light had come on, and the sound of loud voices could be heard. Moments later the burglar reappeared, and this time he was faced with a weapon, as carried by Francine. She was pointing a gun at the burglar, and gesturing to the window.

The sight of a man diving out of a window of his own volition wasn't something I'd actually seen performed in real life. But I had the pleasure of seeing it perform now. For the man didn't have the patience to scurry down the drainpipe. Instead, in his effort to get away from Francine and her gun, he simply jumped out of the window!

"I believe I can fly," Harriet hummed.

Unfortunately the burglar couldn't fly, but as luck would have it his fall was broken by the smooth lawn, made extra soft by the combined efforts of Jackie's family. There was a dull thud as he landed, and for a moment he simply lay there. But then he got up, and staggered away, alive and well. Or at least alive.

"And stay out!" Francine yelled after him.

"He'll live to burgle another day," said Brutus, and he couldn't hide the admiration in his voice.

Burgling is a job like any other, and you had to admit that the man possessed the necessary requisites for this job in the form of nerves of steel and a positive mental attitude, not to mention physical prowess.

"Francine saved us," said Dooley. "If it hadn't been for her, this man would have taken our kibble!"

"No burglar is interested in cat kibble, Dooley," said Brutus.

"He didn't seem particularly interested in my singing either," said Harriet sadly. "He didn't even stick around for my next song."

"He'll be back," I told her.

"You think?" she asked hopefully.

"Of course. He simply cannot stay away."

"I knew it," she said with satisfaction. "I recognize a fan when I see one and this guy is definitely a fan."

"Okay, show's over," I told my friends. "Let's all get some sleep, and be ready for tomorrow, when Francine will meet with Mike Knight."

"How do you plan to get in the room with them?" asked Brutus.

"I have no idea, Brutus. But I'll think of something."

I really wanted to be there when those two met. I had a feeling a lot of the questions we had been asking ourselves were going to be answered. Too bad Odelia was still out of commission, and so was Chase. I glanced up at the window, which Francine had firmly closed. I suddenly had an idea, and wondered if I should risk it.

* * *

THE HOUSE on Harrington Street where Odelia and Chase Kingsley lived was quiet like the proverbial mouse, except for the almost inaudible squeak of the pet flap. For a moment nothing stirred, but then silent footsteps could be heard padding up the stairs. The footsteps paused on the third step, which always creaked a little, but when no response came, the intruder continued his ascent.

Moments later he was in the main bedroom, where Francine Martin lay awake in bed. She had just chased away an intruder, and even though she should be sleeping, her restless mind kept churning and preventing her from finding peace.

Tomorrow was an important day. She was meeting Mike at the house, where an expert would officially determine whether the diary was the genuine article or not. If the expert gave his approval, the diary would change hands and so would a sizable down payment in cash. It was the culmination of months of preparation on her part and that of her associate Brian Seltzer.

She just hoped all of that work would finally pay off.

She closed her eyes and drifted into a fitful sleep.

She didn't notice, therefore, when the intruder traipsed up to the bed. When he heard her even breathing, and saw that her eyelids were closed, he set about his own mission.

Before long he had found what he was looking for.

CHAPTER 34

Mike's car arrived half an hour early, but Francine didn't mind. After a restless night she was ready to get the show on the road. She had a lot riding on this and was hoping the pay-off would be worth it. The driver had rung the bell, and when she opened the door, she thought he looked familiar. He was small, old and wearing suspiciously dark face fuzz. But then it struck her that Mike was probably the kind of person who didn't kick out an old retainer, even if he was obviously past his retirement age.

"How old are you?" she asked as she grabbed her coat and purse.

"Sixty," the chauffeur answered, causing Francine to give him a look of surprise. He didn't look a day under seventy. Then again, some people do look older than their age, after having lived a hard life. Maybe that was the case for this poor fellow.

She followed him out to the car, a shiny black BMW, and got in.

* * *

AFTER WE HAD CONVINCED Gran to impersonate Mike Knight's driver, it didn't take her long to find the appropriate vehicle. She managed to borrow a fine BMW from her old friend Rock Horowitz. The disguise was another matter entirely. She might think she could get away with sticking a beard to her face, but both Dooley and I thought she looked horrible, and Francine would see through the disguise immediately.

But Gran had insisted it was all down to her acting skills, which she possessed in spades. A change of voice, a different posture. She could easily pass for a man, she told us, and clearly it had worked, for even as we patiently waited in the trunk of the car, we could hear Francine's voice as she instructed Gran to take her to the house.

The only thing we hadn't counted on was the company we were forced to keep. The car had only been idling on the road for a minute when all of a sudden the trunk was yanked open and a man crawled in. I recognized him as Brian, the beardless associate Francine had met last night in the field.

He was as surprised to see us as we were to see him. But somehow we managed to find a mode of cohabitation in the limited confines of the trunk. We didn't scratch his eyes out, and he didn't try to choke us. He didn't even give us away, but that was probably due to the fact that he didn't want us to give him away either.

In other words: we were all on a mission, and some form of cooperation naturally occurred.

"What is he doing here, Max?!" Dooley hissed as the car pulled away from the curb and we were on our way.

"I have no idea!" I hissed back.

"Don't scratch me, all right?" Brian said with a touch of trepidation. "I don't like to be scratched."

"We won't scratch you," I told him. "As long as you don't kick us out."

The conditions of this unusual cooperation thus arranged, we proceeded to live together in the back of that car in more or less perfect harmony.

Soon enough, we arrived at our destination. We heard the car doors slam, and next thing we knew, Gran opened the trunk. When she saw Brian, she blinked. But you have to hand it to the old lady: she didn't miss a beat. Instead of panicking, she simply said, "Hi there."

"Hi," said Brian, then quickly crawled out of the trunk and skedaddled, leaving us to stare after him with some surprise.

"Let's go," said Gran, who had no time to waste. She assisted Dooley and myself out of the trunk, then slammed it shut while we hid underneath the vehicle. When we saw Francine's retreating feet from our vantage point, we quickly made to follow.

We were on a mission, and we weren't going to fail!

Francine didn't have to ring the doorbell, for the moment she arrived on the front porch, the door swung open and Mike appeared. Or at least I assumed this was Francine's cousin, since we had never actually laid eyes on the man until that moment.

"Come in," he said, then glanced behind her. "Where is Jim?"

"You mean your driver? I think he said something about parking the car."

"Good," said Mike, and stepped aside to allow his cousin into the house. When he glanced back for a moment, that's when Dooley and I made our move and quickly scooted past him and into the hallway. We only needed a moment to find a suitable hiding place behind a chest of drawers, and patiently awaited further proceedings.

Mike took Francine into a room leading off the hallway, and we tiptoed behind the cousins, hoping to get a front-row seat for the proceedings. As we snuck into the room, we saw it was decorated as a drawing room, with overstuffed green sofas, white curtains framing French windows and plenty of paintings on the walls depicting horses in all shapes and sizes. A glass coffee table groaned under the weight of several art books sporting a horse motif and vases filled with fragrant blooms lent the room a pleasant atmosphere.

As we entered, and quickly scooted underneath the biggest couch, I caught a glimpse of a whiskered man already seated on one of the couches. He was wearing reading glasses and a vague smile on his face.

"Oh, I see you've arrived already," said Francine.

"Yes, I got here about fifteen minutes ago," said the whiskered fellow.

"It was good of you to come all this way, Professor Van Der Beek," said Mike. "I know you're a busy man."

"Oh, nonsense," said the prof. "When Francine told me over the phone that she had come into the possession of a diary belonging to your great-grandfather, I was naturally curious to see it for myself."

"Did you bring the diary?" asked Mike, clearly eager to get down to brass tacks.

"Yes, I did," she said. There was a rustle of fabric, as I assumed the diary was being removed from its resting place, and as I took a peek from under the couch, I saw that a small leather-bound book had been placed on the glass coffee table. It looked pretty old and tattered, with yellowed pages and leather that had turned black with age.

"Oh, dear me," said the prof as he gingerly picked up the specimen. "Now will you look at that?"

Both Francine and Mike were quiet as he studied the booklet, carefully and respectfully turning it over in his hands. He then opened it and began studying its pages. Finally he took a loupe from his vest pocket and took a closer look at the now-famous diary.

I could tell from the way Mike's fingers were twitching that he was nervous about the outcome of this examination of the ancient relic. Francine, on the other hand, looked cool as a cucumber. I wondered what her game was, to be honest. From my close inspection of her room last night I knew she was up to something. But what, exactly? What did she hope to accomplish here today?

Finally the prof must have felt he had kept his audience in suspense long enough, for he placed the diary back inside the box Francine had brought it in, and covered it with the cloth that protected it from the elements. He smiled. "I want to thank you for this rare opportunity," he said. "And to answer your question, Mr. Knight, the diary is genuine. Absolutely genuine."

"Oh, thank God," said Mike, dragging his fingers through his hair. He seemed extremely relieved. "Are you sure, professor?"

"One hundred percent. There's no doubt in my mind that it is the real deal."

Mike produced a sound that was somewhere between a sob and a gasp. For a moment he chewed on his knuckles, his smile something to behold. "Thank you, professor. Thank you so much. You have no idea what this means for my family and me."

"I can only imagine what it must be like to retrieve a valuable personal item like this," said the professor good-naturedly. "To get this rare glimpse into the mind of your ancestor is very gratifying. Very gratifying indeed." He got up with some effort. "And now if you don't mind, I'll leave you to discuss its significance with your cousin, while I take my leave."

"Thank you again, professor," said Mike as he also got up. He pressed an envelope into James Van Der Beek's hands, and as the aged prof briefly checked its contents I saw that it contained plenty of greenbacks. The man's consultant's fee, no doubt.

The professor left the room, and then it was just Mike and Francine.

"I told you it was real," said Francine with a note of triumph in her voice.

"I know, but I had to make sure," said Mike, taking a seat again. "I hope you'll forgive me, but it's important that we put our cooperation on a sound footing from the start." He took a deep breath. "Which means I now owe you one hundred thousand for the diary, correct?"

"Correct," Francine confirmed. Behind me, Dooley was giving me a gentle poke, and when I glanced back, he mouthed, 'One hundred thousand!' I nodded. It was a lot of money. Then again, if this diary provided a clue to the location of that lithium mine, it was well worth the price.

Mike had placed a small attaché case on the table, and now snapped the locks. Inside, bundles of bank notes could be seen, and Francine quickly checked them, then nodded. "Seems fine," she told her cousin.

"And now for the contract," said Mike, and placed a document on the coffee table along with a pen.

"Do you mind if I take this home with me? I would like to consult a lawyer."

Mike smiled. "Don't you trust me?"

"Of course. But I'm no legal beagle. And as you said, it's best if we put this collaboration on a sound footing from the start."

"You're absolutely right," said Mike. "Which is why I have called in the assistance of a lawyer who can advise you." He got up with some alacrity and opened the door. At his sign, a tall man strode in, dressed in a fine charcoal business suit. He was young and handsome but there was something sinister about him.

"I appreciate the gesture, Mike," said Francine. "But I'd prefer to consult my own lawyer, if you don't mind."

The lawyer had closed the door and stood with his back to it, effectively preventing Francine from exiting the room. From the way he was standing he looked more like a bodyguard than a lawyer.

"I'm afraid I do mind," he said. "In fact I mind a lot. Don't you trust me, Francine?" he repeated.

"Oh, I do," she said, and I could tell that an edge had slipped into her voice. "But it's standard business practice to get some independent advice, Mike. You're a businessman. You know this."

For a moment Mike didn't speak. Then he sighed a weary sigh. "Don't take this personally, Francine. I know we've only got acquainted very recently, and if you knew me better you'd know how important family is to me. But fifty percent of whatever that mine yields simply isn't going to cut it for me."

"What are you talking about? We had a deal."

"I know we did. But I'm making some changes."

"What changes?"

Mike nodded to the lawyer, who had unbuttoned his suit jacket. A bulge appeared and before long the glint of the butt of a gun.

"Mike?" said Francine, clearly alarmed by these developments.

"Like I said, nothing personal," said Mike. "But I need that money."

"Okay, so let's renegotiate. How about sixty-forty?"

"How about a hundred percent for me and nothing for you?" Mike suggested, his voice suddenly smooth as silk.

"What?!"

The 'lawyer' had taken the gun out of its holster and was now pointing it directly at Francine. "Move," he growled.

"You're making a mistake, Mike," said Francine.

"I know," said Mike. "But I'm afraid it's inevitable." He grabbed the suitcase from the table and closed it.

"That's my money!"

"Actually you'll find that it's mine," said Mike. He snatched the diary up and tucked it away into the pocket of his coat. "And so is this."

"Are you crazy?"

"Crazy about my family," said Mike with a touch of sadness. "I'd do anything for them." He strode up to his cousin and touched her cheek. "I'm sorry," he said quietly, then quickly left the room.

The gunman had opened one of the French windows and now forced Francine to step out onto the patio. He then poked the gun into her back and directed her toward the side of the house.

"We have to do something, Max!" Dooley said. "He's going to kill her!"

"I know," I said, thinking frantically about how to proceed. I knew Francine had a gun of her own, and hoped she had brought it along. All she needed was a distraction and hopefully she could turn the tables on Mike's henchman.

We hurried out through the French window and saw that Francine was being forced to head in the direction of a large structure that looked like a stable. Probably where Mike kept some of his fine horses.

"He's going to feed her to the horses!" said Dooley.

"Horses don't eat human flesh," I told him. "Do they?"

"If I were you I wouldn't wait to find out, Max."

So we scooted after the duo. And we'd almost caught up with them when suddenly Gran appeared, along with Brian.

For some reason Gran had ditched the beard and was now looking like herself again.

"Who are you?" asked the gunman, surprised.

And as he was thus distracted, that's when I decided to jump the man, planting my nails into his back. I'd never actually performed such a move before, but we had been watching a martial arts movie not so long ago, and the leading man's signature move had somehow stayed with me. Now seemed like a perfect time to try it out on a living, breathing person.

The reaction of the gunman was instantaneous. He screamed like a wounded kitten, and as he threw up his arms to get rid of the sudden monster that was attacking him from behind, Francine deftly caught his gun, and when finally the gunman came to his senses, he was staring down the barrel of his own weapon.

I dropped down to the ground again, mission accomplished, and started licking my nails to get rid of the stench of this nasty human.

"FBI," Francine suddenly shouted. "You're under arrest, buddy."

Gran blinked. "FBI? What did I miss?"

Quite a lot, as it turned out.

CHAPTER 35

It hadn't taken Vesta long to get wise to the fact that the mystery man concealed in the trunk of her car was up to no good. And so she had decided to keep an eye on him while her cats kept an eye on Francine.

Time was of the essence, since Mike Knight's real driver, arriving some thirty minutes after she had picked up Francine, would at some point realize that something was wrong and would phone his boss, alerting Mike to the presence of an impostor in their midst.

Gran's stowaway had disappeared inside a boxy structure that could only be the horse stable, and even though she wasn't overly fond of horses, she still figured she better stay hot on the man's tail or else.

She snuck in through the high stable door and it took a moment for her eyes to adjust to the relative obscurity. Glancing around, she could hear the horses moving restlessly. They must have felt the presence of this stranger and didn't like it one bit. Several of the horses had appeared in the doors of their stalls and were glancing out at her. She wondered where the man had disappeared to, and as she looked around, and snuck along the central corridor where the different horse stalls looked out onto, she became aware of their piercing eyes and curious gazes. Several of the horses neighed and she now regretted not having one of the cats with her. No doubt they'd be able to understand what they were saying and could translate.

But as it was, she simply had to rely on her own instincts. She had reached the end, and saw that a light was on in what looked like an office. Sneaking closer, she glanced in, and saw that her illegal passenger was checking a file cabinet, rifling through the different folders. He grimaced, then turned his attention to the computer on a desk, and took a seat. And as he was busy inspecting the contents of the computer, suddenly a smile appeared on his face, a face that wasn't much to look at, to be honest. In fact the man looked like a hardened criminal, scars and tattoos and all. He took out his phone and started snapping pictures of the screen, presumably having found what he was looking for.

She wondered how she should proceed. The guy might not be Mr. Handsome, but he was pretty sturdily built and she was clearly no match for him. She now wished she had told her son about this mission. But Max had told her it was strictly a reconnaissance mission, and they needed to collect information before they involved Alec. Clearly the man inside that office was of the same mind, since collecting data was all he cared about.

She was about to retreat when her foot nudged a bucket filled with feed for the horses. It toppled over with a loud clanking sound, and suddenly the man was next to her, giving her the once-over. He looked a lot less friendly than before, when they had come face to face the first time.

"It's not what it looks like," she managed to say.

"It looks like you're spying on me," the man said.

She decided bluster was the best response. "And it looks

like you're spying on Mike Knight," she said, drawing herself up to her full height, which was still a full head shorter than this fellow.

Suddenly his eyes narrowed, and as his hand attached itself to her beard, there was a sort of tearing sound, and the beard came off in his hand. He stared at her, astonishment written all over his ugly face.

"But... you're a crone!" he cried.

"Who are you calling a crone!" she said, and before she could stop herself, slapped him across the face, hard. "Have some respect for your elders, sonny Jim. What would your mother think?"

"My mother?" he said. "What about my grandmother!"

"Age is just a number. So what if I am a little older than the average driver? I'm not ready to retire yet."

"If you're a driver I'm Brad Pitt. Who are you?"

It was clear the gig was up. "Vesta Muffin at your service."

"Vesta Muffin? You mean you're Odelia Kingsley's grandmother?"

"That's correct. And who are you?"

He thought for a moment, his eyes turning a little shifty. She was just about to give him another slap for good measure when he said, "What if I told you that I'm law enforcement?"

"I'd tell you you're a lousy liar."

"No, but I am. Brian Seltzer. DEA."

And he would possibly have said more, if not a loud conversation carried out outside had intruded upon this moment. They exchanged a look, then hurried to go see what was going on. Vesta because she was worried about her cats, and Brian presumably because he was worried about Francine. Was she also law enforcement? she thought. If so, that woman had a lot of explaining to do!

* * *

Even though he should have felt relieved, Mike wasn't. He liked Francine, and regretted having to get rid of her. But it couldn't be helped. He was in urgent need of that money, after having been dealt a few rough hands lately. Half of that lithium wasn't good enough. He needed all of it—every last cent.

After twenty minutes had passed, he figured the coast was clear, and decided to take a stroll to the stables to check on his precious horses. Horses were in his blood. Always had been. Even though his family had made their money in potash mining, from a young age his great passion in life had been horses. He bred them, raced them, sold and bought them. His favorite was Man Friday. What a specimen. The stallion had won him plenty of prize money, and even more in stud fees. He was getting a little long in the tooth now, but still fetched a pretty penny.

He slipped into the stables through the back door and breathed in that very particular scent he loved so much. That pungent smell of horse manure never failed to bring back some great memories. And as he strolled past the horses, they whinnied in recognition of their master. When he arrived at Fury's stall, though, he frowned. Emily's horse wasn't there.

Immediately he took out his phone and called his stable manager. "Rick, hi. Listen, do you know where Fury is? He's not in his stall."

"Your wife took him."

"My wife!"

"Yeah. Something about a trip to Westchester County?"

"Impossible. Yvonne and Emily are in Manhattan this weekend, shopping."

"That's not what she told me, boss. She specifically told

me that Emily was so excited about entering her very first competition. Must be the horse show in Pleasantville. It's open to contestants of all ages."

He glanced wildly around himself. This couldn't be happening. Not Fury, not now! "When is the competition?" he demanded.

"Um, today, I think." He checked something, then confirmed, "Yep. She's supposed to compete today. What's the matter, boss? Something wrong?"

"No, it's fine," he said quickly. "Everything's all right." He disconnected and thought hard, his jaw working. Then he pulled up his wife's number and dialed. It went straight to voicemail. She must have turned off her phone so she could focus on Emily's competition. He tried Emily's phone, but that was switched off as well.

And as he walked out of the stables, suddenly he was met with a chilling sight: Francine was pointing a gun at him. Over to her left Bill was standing, handcuffed and giving the man next to him dirty looks. The man didn't seem to mind. On the contrary, he was grinning like an idiot. An old woman was also there, and two cats. What was going on!

"Hands in the air, Mike," said Francine. "Now!"

"Please," he said. "My daughter is in terrible danger."

"You're in terrible danger if you don't do as I say." She was holding up a badge now, he saw. "DEA," she said as she flashed the badge. "Mike Knight, you're under arrest for—"

"It's her horse!" he insisted. "She can't enter that competition. Please, you have to listen to me!"

"What's all this about your daughter and a horse?" asked the old lady as she approached.

"It's Fury," he said, licking beads of sweat from his upper lip. "If she enters him into that competition..."

"What?"

"He'll collapse and he will die."

CHAPTER 36

Emily was having the time of her life. This was what she had dreamed of all her life. Ever since she was a little girl she had loved horses. Of course she hadn't been allowed to ride one until her parents considered her old enough. First she'd owned a pony, and even though she had adored her pony, it wasn't enough. What she wanted was to ride a real horse. A horse like Fury: strong and fast and ever so graceful. It had taken a lot of begging and pleading, but finally her dad had relented. Fury was an older horse, sedate and calm. But to her he was like a rocket, and feeling all that power underneath the saddle had given her the rush of a lifetime. So she had taken to riding him every day, under the tutelage of a trainer.

The fervent wish to enter the world of show jumping had come later, after she had gone to see a competition with her mom. The Hamptons Classic Horse Show was one of the biggest equestrian events of the year, with horses and riders coming from all over the country. All the pieces of the puzzle had finally come together for her that day. This was what she wanted to do with her life. This was what she was born for!

But no amount of pleading had convinced her dad to let her enter Fury into a competition. She was too young and it was far too dangerous. She could get hurt, or Fury could be injured. Her mom had other ideas. She could see her daughter's passion for horse riding, and didn't want to stop her from pursuing her dream. She had read somewhere that in order to become a contestant you have to start young, and twelve seemed like the perfect age to enter her first competition. She wasn't going to win, not on Fury, but it was a great first experience, and would give her a glimpse at her future self, riding other, more powerful horses and entering actual competitions. And who knows, one day she might even compete at that very same Hamptons Classic, or go to the Olympics and become an actual Olympic equestrian!

Mom was almost as excited as she was, or perhaps even more so, and so was Sylvie, her best friend. Too bad Sylv would never be able to ride a horse herself, but she said that was fine. The enjoyment Emily got from the experience was enough for her, and she had almost just as much fun as her friend.

It was almost Emily's turn, and she could feel the butterflies in her tummy. It wouldn't be long now, and if all went according to plan she would put down a decent time and hopefully not make too many mistakes. Every time Fury knocked down a pole, points would be deducted, and also when he refused to jump one of the obstacles. There weren't as many obstacles as in an actual show jumping competition, the ones governed by the US Equestrian Federation, and many of the contestants were under the age of twelve, which made Emily wonder why she hadn't been allowed to start training sooner. But the main thing was that she had made it this far. And as her mother didn't stop reminding her in a bid to temper her expectations: the purpose today wasn't to win, but to gain experience. And that's exactly what she intended to do.

Fury seemed restless, so she placed a hand on his nose. He breathed in her scent and softly neighed.

"It's fine, buddy," she said. "You're going to be great."

But he seemed more nervous than usual, even though they had been practicing this exact type of course for months, making sure they did when her dad wasn't watching too closely, lest he got nervous. Which wasn't hard, for he spent a lot of time at the office. The only ones who knew were her trainer, Mom and Sylvie. And the stable manager Rick, of course. That couldn't be helped, since he was in charge of the horses, and had to arrange transportation for Fury. But by the time he told Dad the race would be over.

She glanced out at the obstacle course with shiny eyes. This was it. Another five minutes and she would be out there, doing what she was made to do. "Oh, Fury, it's simply going to be glorious!" she whispered.

The horse moved its lips, and somehow she had a feeling he was sad. She wondered why that could be. Usually she could sense what was troubling Fury, but today she couldn't. Was he nervous, or coming down with something? Rick would know. Nobody knew as much about horses as Rick. He was the master.

One of the assistants officiating the competition gave her the sign that it was time for her to enter the ring. They were introduced, and then it was time to take her position and get ready for the starting bell.

She could see her mom and Sylvie among the spectators nearby, and she waved at them. They waved back, and she could tell that they were as excited as she was.

She mounted Fury, and placed her hands lightly on the leads, her booted feet in the stirrups, mentally visualizing the course. She knew it by heart. Every obstacle. Every jump. It wouldn't be long now. Any second…

Suddenly a man appeared by her side. It was the same official who'd given her the go-ahead. He was accompanied by a second man she had never seen before. He looked a little rumpled, she thought, as if he'd been sleeping in his car. Both men wore tense expressions on their faces, and the official had placed a hand on Fury's lead, yanking it down and making sure they weren't going anywhere. Then he looked up and said, "I'm sorry, sweetheart. But I can't let you ride today. Better get down."

"But… why?"

He shook his head. "I'm not sure."

He glanced down Fury's flank. A third person came hurrying over, a medical bag in hand. He was a doctor, and started examining Fury even as Emily was helped down from her high perch.

The doctor touched his hand to Fury's abdomen, and the horse suddenly whinnied loudly and kicked out with his rear leg.

The doctor exchanged a nod with the official.

"Your horse isn't fit," the latter told Emily.

Her mom came hurrying up, pushing Sylvie's wheelchair.

"What's wrong?" asked Mom.

"I don't know," said Emily. "They say I can't compete."

"But why?"

More people gathered around, and Fury was quickly led away. Emily tried to reach him, to comfort him, for he seemed so upset. But they kept her away from him. And it was as she jostled with the men holding her back that she collided with Sylvie's wheelchair. It almost toppled over, and Sylvie fell out onto the ground. From the pocket of her jacket something fell. Sylvie cried out in distress and tried to grab the item. But Emily beat her to it. She picked it up and stared at it.

It was a firecracker. And when her eyes met her friend's, she could see that guilt was written all over her face. Then she looked away.

And that's when the awful truth came home to her.

CHAPTER 37

"Sylvie tried to kill Emily?" asked Harriet.

"Not kill her," I said. "Cripple her. So they would both be in a wheelchair. She was afraid that Emily would move on, become ever more popular and successful in life, and forget all about her friend. So she figured if she threw a firecracker and spooked Fury, Emily would be thrown off during one of the jumps and make a bad fall and end up in a wheelchair, just like Sylvie, and that way they'd be friends forever."

"It sounds a little delusional," said Harriet.

"It sounds psychotic," Brutus grunted.

"She wasn't thinking straight," I said.

"Still," said Harriet. "I don't think I'd want a friend like Sylvie. Imagine having a sleepover with her trying to smother her friend with a pillow because she might not want to be friends anymore?" She shivered. "Good thing they stopped that race."

"Yeah, well," I said. "That was for a different reason altogether." After the race had been canceled, the doctor examining Fury, under instructions from Francine and one of

Francine's DEA colleagues, who had been keeping an eye on the competition, had discovered a couple of pounds of cocaine inside the horse's stomach. The poor animal had been forced to swallow the stuff in small packets and was going to be transported to Miami, Florida that day, where the drugs would be extracted again. Only Mike didn't know his wife and daughter had different plans for Fury. If those packets had burst, the animal wouldn't have survived, which was what Mike was afraid would happen if his daughter rode Fury in the competition. If he collapsed making a jump, Emily could have died alongside her precious horse.

"What I don't understand," said Harriet, "is why Mike would take that chance. I thought he was a successful businessman? Why become a drug smuggler all of a sudden?"

"Because business wasn't good," I said. "It hadn't been good for a long time. After they were forced to close the mine, Mike's father invested his money in several different ventures. A chain of restaurants, for instance, but unfortunately a recession put a stop to that. Mike also tried his hand at various financial endeavors, but some of his riskier investments had failed, and so he was on the verge of going under. Which is when the lucrative offer came to become a mule for the drug mafia. They liked his stable of horses, and figured there was money to be made. So they had him smuggle the drugs in the horses' trailers, saddles, anything. Mike's horses entered competitions in different South-American countries, and when they crossed the border into the US they usually carried a little extra weight. Only the DEA became suspicious and started watching him. Which is when Mike decided to put the stuff inside the horses instead."

"Yikes," said Brutus. "Imagine having to swallow that stuff."

We were on the porch swing in Marge and Tex's backyard. The human contingent was enjoying a nice barbecue and so was the rest of us. The story had attracted a lot of attention, especially after Odelia published her article revealing the sting operation that had brought down a prominent member of Hampton Cove society. The headline had read, 'How I Welcomed a Drug Enforcer into my Home.' The drug enforcer being Francine, of course. Though it had taken a while for her to reveal her true identity.

"So who was it that poisoned Chase?" asked Dooley.

"That was Brian Seltzer. Turns out he's Francine's partner at the DEA. And he did it without consulting Francine. If he had, she would have told him that drugging a fellow officer was out of the question."

"But why did he do it?" asked Harriet.

"A couple of years ago Brian participated in a joint operation with the NYPD back when Chase was still on the force. So they met a few times. And since he wasn't sure if Chase had also met Francine, he decided not to take any chances and slip something into Chase's water bottle. By the time he woke up, Mike would be behind bars and the case would be closed. But of course he hadn't counted on the fact that Chase would also swallow half a sleeping pill. The combined effect put him in an extended coma, and risked his life."

"I hope this guy Brian will be reprimanded," Brutus growled. He didn't take kindly to people drugging his beloved human, even if they were DEA agents. "The guy is a loose cannon, Max. A loose cannon!"

"I know, I know," I said soothingly. Fortunately Chase had received a clean bill of health, and would suffer no long-term effects from the ordeal.

Brian hadn't meant to put Chase in the hospital. But when he selected our home as a possible place for Francine to hide from the people following her, it was imperative that Chase was out of the picture for the time being. As it was, they were absolutely correct in their determination that Francine's life was in danger.

"I still don't understand why they selected Odelia," Dooley said. "Why us? Why our home?"

"Well, as it happens it was actually a previous assignment that put us on the DEA agents' radar. The assignment involved staking out a house not all that far from Harrington Street. Which is how Jackie, our mole friend, first came face to face with Francine and Brian Seltzer—back then still sporting a beard. To bide their time while they watched the house of a suspected drug dealer and member of a notorious motorcycle gang, they took to reading the *Hampton Cove Gazette*, and followed Odelia's exploits with interest. And so when they were tasked with organizing a sting operation to catch Mike Knight, and Francine needed a place to lie low, Odelia's name popped up."

"So what's going to happen now?" asked Harriet.

"Mike has been arrested, and has been asked to turn state's evidence. He has a lot of interesting information to impart about the people he was working for. Chances are that he will cooperate. If only to stand a chance at one day being reunited with his family again."

"Odd that he would do all this to save his family from financial ruin," said Brutus, "but end up almost killing his own daughter."

"Yeah, I very much doubt whether his wife will ever forgive him," I said.

"She didn't know?" asked Harriet.

"No, she didn't. Mike's father did. He claims he didn't, but once Mike finally starts talking, I'm sure the truth will be revealed."

"So what about the guy who tried to break into our home?" asked Harriet. "Was he also a DEA agent?"

"No, he was actually working for the drug mafia. They

were suspicious when Francine contacted Mike and told him about the lithium. Mostly they were afraid that Mike would become financially solvent again, and wouldn't need them anymore. They had big plans for him. Not only to use his stable of horses as drug mules, but also as a way of laundering money. They could use Mike to buy and sell horses, and also use them for breeding purposes. People will pay a lot of money for a good stallion and not all of that money is paid through official channels, and so it's a business the mafia definitely wanted to be a part of."

"So they figured they'd keep an eye on Francine," said Brutus.

I nodded. "They wanted to know who she was. And if she really did own that diary, as she claimed. If so, they would have grabbed it. Then they could force Mike to go into business with them operating a lithium mine. It would only serve to increase their hold over him, something Mike was desperate to get out of. He needed that mine and its proceeds to pay off his debts and get out from under the mob's thumb."

"How did he get involved with the mob in the first place?" asked Brutus. "I would have thought a man like Mike would know better than to sell his soul to these people?"

"Like I said, he was in a terrible financial position, and stood to lose everything: the house, his standing in the community, the fancy school Emily was going to, the clubs Yvonne was a member of. So when someone offered to tide him over in exchange for using his horse business once or twice, he didn't see the danger. Of course once they got him involved, there was no escape. They owned him."

"I almost feel sorry for the guy," said Brutus with a grimace. "Until I realize that he actually stuffed cocaine inside his daughter's horse and ordered to have Francine killed!"

"That wasn't very nice of him," Dooley agreed.

"Not nice!" Brutus cried. "How about criminal!"

"No need to shout," said Dooley, rubbing his ear. "I can hear you loud and clear, Brutus."

"So the diary," said Harriet. "Was it real? And is Francine really Mike's distant cousin?"

"No, she's not," I said. "And the diary is a fake."

"But that professor said it was real," said Dooley.

"That professor was also a DEA agent," I said. "The whole point of the diary was to get close enough to Mike so they could take a good look at his business and his files. That's what Brian was doing. Francine's job was to distract her so-called cousin and smuggle Brian into the place, which was pretty heavily guarded, as you can imagine. Then once Brian had managed to sneak a look at Mike's books, and positively determine they were cooked, they had enough evidence to put Mike behind bars."

Dooley laughed. "Why would anyone want to cook a book, Max? That must taste awful!"

"It's just an expression, Dooley," I said. I glanced down at the medal I'd been awarded. It was nice and shiny, and instead of pinning it to my chest, as is customary, Francine had hung it around my neck, telling Odelia I deserved it, for I had saved her life by jumping on top of Mike's goon. She did ask Odelia whether it was true that she could talk to cats. Something Odelia had vehemently denied. All in all I had the distinct impression that Francine's aversion to cats had somewhat mellowed. We were clearly growing on her.

"Nice medal," Brutus said, a touch of envy in his voice.

"Yeah, it's very shiny," Harriet agreed. "Where are you going to put it, Max?

"Oh, I don't know," I said. "Odelia will probably find a nice place for it."

"Is it real gold?" asked Dooley, carefully reaching out a paw to touch it.

"I doubt it," I said. "But it's always nice to be appreciated."

"Looks like all's well that ends well," said Harriet, releasing a profound breath of relief. "Even our ringworm is clearing up. So pretty soon we'll all get a clean bill of health, you guys. How great is that?"

"Pretty great," I agreed with a smile.

Pretty much the entire cat population of our small town had been treated against this pernicious fungus, and the results were excellent. Our period of forced exile was coming to an end, and very soon now the hugging could recommence. Not that I'm a big fan of being hugged, mind you, but it's still nicer than being shunned, which we had been to some extent, due to our predicament. Especially Grace had a hard time staying away from us. The kid is a natural hugger, and likes nothing better than to squeeze us and caress us with her grubby hands and generally treat us as her personal plush animals.

The blame for the ringworm epidemic would probably never be placed on one single person or cat, and that was fine. These things happen, and the important thing is to catch them in time and get rid of them before they can do any real damage.

I closed my eyes to get some rest. It had been an eventful couple of days, and I was long overdue for a nice long nap.

"Max?" asked Dooley.

"Mh?" I said, reluctant to open my eyes again.

"Do you think Odelia and Chase will allow Jackie and her family to stay in our backyard?"

"Sure. Why not?" I said.

"Well, because of that," he said.

I opened my eyes, and saw that several molehills had appeared on Tex's nice lawn. They were popping up at a rapid pace. Tex had noticed the same thing, for his jaw dropped and he shouted, "Moles!"

"I read that moles are good for the lawn," said Marge. "They provide air to the soil and get rid of bugs."

"Nonsense!" Tex bellowed. "Whoever told you that is a two-faced quack!"

"Oh, will you look at that?" said Marge. "How cute."

Jackie's head had popped out of one of the molehills closest to Tex, and gave us a wave and a wink.

We waved back.

Tex followed the interaction with a baleful eye. "It's a conspiracy!" he cried. "They're out to destroy my backyard!"

"I think they're just passing through," said Marge, and gestured to the series of molehills tracking a clear path across the backyard in the direction of the Trapper backyard.

Tex watched this with widening eyes, then laughed. "Go on!" he said, urging the mole family on with word and deed. "Plenty of good grub next door!"

"Oh, honey," said Marge, shaking her head. "You really shouldn't encourage them."

But Tex was grinning from ear to ear. "Oh, it's all right," he said, relaxing again. "Moles are fine. They provide air to the soil and get rid of bugs. It's all to the good."

Marge shared a look with her daughter, and they both rolled their eyes. "Whatever you say, Dad," said Odelia.

"Do you think Jackie will have enough to eat?" asked Dooley, worried as he watched the family of moles traverse our backyard and disappear beneath the hedge. "She has a lot of mouths to feed, after all."

"I'm sure they have all the food they need," I said. Once they were done with Ted Trapper's backyard, they had an entire field where they could eat to their heart's content. And who knows, they might be back one day, and start the circle all over again. I didn't mind. Jackie was good people, and so was Dave.

And so I finally closed my eyes and fell into a deep, relaxing sleep.

That nice shiny medal clutched between my paws said I deserved it.

THE END

Thanks for reading! If you want to know when a new Nic Saint book comes out, sign up for Nic's mailing list: nicsaint.com/news

ABOUT NIC

Nic has a background in political science and before being struck by the writing bug worked odd jobs around the world (including but not limited to massage therapist in Mexico, gardener in Italy, restaurant manager in India, and Berlitz teacher in Belgium).

When he's not writing he enjoys curling up with a good (comic) book, watching British crime dramas, French comedies or Nancy Meyers movies, sampling pastry (apple cake!), pasta and chocolate (preferably the dark variety), twisting himself into a pretzel doing morning yoga, going for a run, and spoiling his big red tomcat Tommy.

He lives with his wife (and aforementioned cat) in a small village smack dab in the middle of absolutely nowhere and is probably writing his next 'Mysteries of Max' book right now.

www.nicsaint.com

ALSO BY NIC SAINT

The Mysteries of Max

Purrfect Murder

Purrfectly Deadly

Purrfect Revenge

Purrfect Heat

Purrfect Crime

Purrfect Rivalry

Purrfect Peril

Purrfect Secret

Purrfect Alibi

Purrfect Obsession

Purrfect Betrayal

Purrfectly Clueless

Purrfectly Royal

Purrfect Cut

Purrfect Trap

Purrfectly Hidden

Purrfect Kill

Purrfect Boy Toy

Purrfectly Dogged

Purrfectly Dead

Purrfect Saint

Purrfect Advice

Purrfect Passion

A Purrfect Gnomeful

Purrfect Cover

Purrfect Patsy

Purrfect Son

Purrfect Fool

Purrfect Fitness

Purrfect Setup

Purrfect Sidekick

Purrfect Deceit

Purrfect Ruse

Purrfect Swing

Purrfect Cruise

Purrfect Harmony

Purrfect Sparkle

Purrfect Cure

Purrfect Cheat

Purrfect Catch

Purrfect Design

Purrfect Life

Purrfect Thief

Purrfect Crust

Purrfect Bachelor

Purrfect Double

Purrfect Date

Purrfect Hit

Purrfect Baby

Purrfect Mess

Purrfect Paris

Purrfect Model

Purrfect Slug

Purrfect Match

Purrfect Game

Purrfect Bouquet

Purrfect Home

Purrfectly Slim

Purrfect Nap

Purrfect Yacht

Purrfect Scam

Purrfect Fury

The Mysteries of Max Collections

Collection 1 (Books 1-3)

Collection 2 (Books 4-6)

Collection 3 (Books 7-9)

Collection 4 (Books 10-12)

Collection 5 (Books 13-15)

Collection 6 (Books 16-18)

Collection 7 (Books 19-21)

Collection 8 (Books 22-24)

Collection 9 (Books 25-27)

Collection 10 (Books 28-30)

Collection 11 (Books 31-33)

Collection 12 (Books 34-36)

Collection 13 (Books 37-39)

Collection 14 (Books 40-42)

Collection 15 (Books 43-45)

Collection 16 (Books 46-48)

Collection 17 (Books 49-51)

Collection 18 (Books 52-54)

Collection 19 (Books 55-57)

Collection 20 (Books 58-60)

The Mysteries of Max Big Collections

Big Collection 1 (Books 1-10)

Big Collection 2 (Books 11-20)

The Mysteries of Max Short Stories

Collection 1 (Stories 1-3)

Collection 2 (Stories 4-7)

Nora Steel

Murder Retreat

The Kellys

Murder Motel

Death in Suburbia

Emily Stone

Murder at the Art Class

Washington & Jefferson

First Shot

Alice Whitehouse

Spooky Times

Spooky Trills

Spooky End

Spooky Spells

Ghosts of London

Between a Ghost and a Spooky Place

Public Ghost Number One

Ghost Save the Queen

Box Set 1 (Books 1-3)

A Tale of Two Harrys

Ghost of Girlband Past

Ghostlier Things

Charleneland

Deadly Ride

Final Ride

Neighborhood Witch Committee

Witchy Start

Witchy Worries

Witchy Wishes

Saffron Diffley

Crime and Retribution

Vice and Verdict

Felonies and Penalties (Saffron Diffley Short 1)

The B-Team

Once Upon a Spy

Tate-à-Tate

Enemy of the Tates

Ghosts vs. Spies

The Ghost Who Came in from the Cold

Witchy Fingers

Witchy Trouble

Witchy Hexations

Witchy Possessions

Witchy Riches

Box Set 1 (Books 1-4)

The Mysteries of Bell & Whitehouse

One Spoonful of Trouble

Two Scoops of Murder

Three Shots of Disaster

Box Set 1 (Books 1-3)

A Twist of Wraith

A Touch of Ghost

A Clash of Spooks

Box Set 2 (Books 4-6)

The Stuffing of Nightmares

A Breath of Dead Air

An Act of Hodd

Box Set 3 (Books 7-9)

A Game of Dons

Standalone Novels

When in Bruges

The Whiskered Spy

ThrillFix

Homejacking

The Eighth Billionaire

The Wrong Woman

Lightning Source UK Ltd.
Milton Keynes UK
UKHW010152240123
415813UK00001B/91

9 789464 446517